Wisconsin Logging Camp, 1921

T0097892

Wisconsin Logging Camp, 1921

A Boy's Extraordinary First Year in America Working as a "Chickadee"

James Bastian

trails books

AN IMPRINT OF BOWER HOUSE

DENVER

This is a work of fiction. Names, characters, places, and incidents are products of the author's imagination or are used fictitiously and are not construed as real. Any resemblance to actual events, locales, organizations, or persons, living or dead, is entirely coincidental.

Wisconsin Logging Camp, 1921. Copyright ©2016 by James Bastian. All rights reserved. No part of this book may be used or reproduced in any manner whatsoever without written permission except in the case of brief quotations embodied in critical articles and reviews. For information, contact Bower House: BowerHouseBooks.com.

Printed in Canada
Text Design: D. K. Luraas
Editorial Director: Mira Perrizo

Special thanks to: Mike Monte, Crandon, WI; German Settlement History Inc., Ogema, WI; and the Forest County Historical Museum

Cover Photo: Dated 1925, from the Forest County Historical Museum, Linnemann Collection Accession, #2013.10.

Library of Congress Control Number: 2015953208
Paperback ISBN: 978-1-934553-54-1
Ebook ISBN: 978-1-934553-82-4

10 9 8 7 6 5 4 3 2

To Carol

1

It's January 4, 1945. I'm in a field hospital a few miles east of the Rhine River. Just returned from a stroll around the ward, assisted by the U.S. Army's largest nurse, Miss Schwartz. She would probably say that she was big-boned or Rubenesque, but I think burly would be more accurate. Frankly I'm happy it's her. She always has a smile and is a real sweetheart, but more importantly, she is the only nurse around here with the strength to hold me up enough to take the load off my sore feet while we walk.

After plopping me on my bed, she is full of high praise. "Nice to see your tootsies aren't as black as they were yesterday, Lieutenant," she called over her broad shoulder as she marched to the next bed. I like her, but I've had a soft spot for nurses ever since I was a kid.

I need a nap, but General Robert LaBrey and two aides come around the blanket hung on a rope blocking my view of some poor bastard just brought in with the right side of his face blown away. The larger of the two aides hands the general one of the dozen small boxes he's carrying. Without looking at the aide, the general takes the box and thrusts it at me.

"Congratulations Lieutenant Heinlein, you're receiving the Purple Heart for a shrapnel wound and frozen feet received during the Battle of the Bulge. I would love to lift a glass of cognac with you from the case we liberated in Lyon, but your doctor seems to advise against that."

"Thank you, General, I would have enjoyed that drink."
I took the box and hoped he would turn his fat ass around
and leave me to my nap.

"You know Will, when you first came out of O.C.S., you
really didn't seem cut out for the army. You weren't, and still
aren't, a 'by the book' officer. Broke a few rules if I remember. But I knew I could always count on your company, just
like at the Bulge. Overrun by the Krauts, hit in the side by
shrapnel, and damn the next afternoon your platoon and
Lieutenant Williams are counterattacking. It was hard for us
at HQ to figure out just what was happening."

"We didn't have many options, General."

What he forgot to mention was that the reason HQ didn't
know what was happening is that LaBrey and pals were
running around with their heads up their asses.

"I appreciate you stopping by, General. I should get a
little rest so I can get out of here and make room for the next
bleeder."

"Happy to come by, Will. You'll be back with your boys
soon enough."

"Good to see you, General," I lied. I rolled on my good
side hoping he'd take the hint.

"You know, Will, I read the reports on the Bulge. I was at
HQ when they hit us. Gettin' a little R and R. What the hell
happened out there when the Krauts threw everything at us?"

"Not much to tell, General. The Krauts just rolled over
us with Panzers. It was at zero two hundred and blizzard
conditions. We were hunkered down in foxholes, really just
depressions in the snow. The ground was like concrete. We
couldn't hack our way in more than a couple of inches. We
heard them coming, but didn't realize they weren't ours until they were right on us. We took ten casualties, mostly from
the Panzers crushing our guys as they rolled over our position. At sunup, it was twenty below. I wasn't about to have
my men sit there and freeze to death, so we just followed the
Krauts back to our lines. Once I figured out where our guys

Battle of the Bulge. *(Braun, USA, public domain)*

were we shot our way through. It was so goddamn cold I didn't even know I was hit until I got back to our lines."

I am not going to tell that asshole that every time I close my eyes I see those goddamn Panzers coming at us. They hit us at night and didn't shell us with screamie-meamies before they attacked. They wanted to surprise us and they did. We couldn't see them until they started shooting. Each muzzle blast lit up the field like lightning. It lit just for an instant then black, creating the impression of a flickering old movie—like a bad horror movie that I had to live through. We only had grenades and bazookas. Nothing heavy enough to knock out a top-of-the-line German tank. At least I lived through it. I'll never forget those images, or the shouts of our guys getting crushed, and the Kraut infantry chasing behind the tanks shooting indiscriminately into our foxholes as they ran by. Then, just like that it was over. The Panzer

Division kept moving. They wanted to break through our main lines and didn't want to waste time cleaning us up.

"Were your feet frozen then, too?"

"Ironically no. Once we got back, some of the guys and I flopped down around a fire that an armor unit built to keep warm. Feet facing the fire, I laid back and fell asleep. Woke up three hours later with frozen feet and a lot of pain in my side where I had gotten hit. My feet were right in front of the fire for Christ's sake. Anyway, should be outta here soon."

"Can't blame you for getting frozen feet. A lot of men can't cope with the cold, much less work, sleep, and fight in knee-deep snow every day for a week. Guess you learned a lesson out there, soldier. I suspect you won't let that happen again."

"I sure did learn a lesson, General. Thanks again for stoppin' in to see me."

It was all I could do to keep from kicking the son-of-a-bitch in the balls, frozen foot and all. The moron didn't have any idea what he was talking about. I spent more time in knee-deep snow at temperatures twenty and thirty below zero when I was a kid than that asshole has in his fifty years of avoiding discomfort. But I think I'll keep that thought to myself and instead focus on improving my day—by getting rid of him.

"Well, you get yourself healed up pronto, Lieutenant. We need you for the push into Berlin."

With that I nodded. He saluted. I weakly lifted my hand. He turned, waited for his aides to begin marching, and finally moved on to a bed down the aisle.

I wasn't tired anymore. Still pissed about LaBrey. *Wouldn't it have been nice if I had worked in snow and cold before?* I did every day for the better part of a year when I was eight years old. That was 1921.

You know what's funny? The year before that, I was living not forty miles from this field hospital. I was a German kid, whose father died fighting in the German army during

World War I. Now I'm back, but this time my sorry ass is trying to kill Germans, maybe even some Heinlein's.

A lot has happened since I left Germany as a kid, of course. But you know how certain events in your life are seared in your memory? Like the sight of those Panzers coming at us. Every detail. Well that's how that first year after leaving Germany was for me. The whole damn year, including the months I worked outside every day during a Wisconsin winter.

I was still seven when I left Germany with my mother. I turned eight a couple of days after my mother died from influenza on the ship coming over. I arrived in New York an orphan and unable to reach my uncle and his family, who were already in the States. Seems they moved and the letter they sent my mother with their new address never arrived.

I was fortunate to run into a couple of Polish brothers who were willing to help me. Not just help but took care of me like a little brother. I was lucky, very lucky. I couldn't have had better mentors or role models than Michael and Deiter. In fact, later that year I became their business partner.

It seems funny saying I had business partners when I was eight. But that is exactly what happened. A junior partner, but I owned shares in the business. Still do. What a year, October 1920 to September 1921. It started when I was orphaned, and then I became a Chickadee. I hated that name. By the end of that year I became part of a family again and finally got my friends to stop calling me Chickadee.

In between, I was stabbed two days after I was released from a flu sanatorium in New York, I helped moonshiners, killed a logger, was a partner in a logging company, and oh yeah, spent an entire winter in knee-deep snow at twenty below working as a Chickadee. It seems like last month, not twenty-three years ago.

2

Chickadees scraped horse shit off iced trails so the horse-drawn sleds carrying logs from the forest would slide easily. If the runners on the sled struck any debris— branches or horse apples frozen on the track—the load would lurch. Those sleds were stacked high with twenty-five to thirty, two-ton logs held in place by a couple of chains. It didn't take much for those logs to snap a chain and go rollin' all over kingdom come. Chickadees cleared the runs every morning before sunup to make sure that didn't happen.

At the time I hated it when those son-of-bitches called me Chickadee. I couldn't understand why they wouldn't call me by my name, Wilhelm Heinlein, or Will, or Hiney, which is what they called Germans. Anything would have been better than being called a tiny chirping bird.

I arrived at the camp a displaced, spoiled, orphaned kid, completely unprepared and unfit for that place. I was frightened—without a family, small and weak—I guess I was like a Chickadee.

At first being a Chickadee was a real struggle. I was bossed, bullied, and incessantly teased by the loggers. Eventually I got used to it and took some pride in being part of a logging camp, except when they called me Chickadee and rubbed my nose in the fact that I had in every sense the shittiest job in camp. It was my boot camp to life.

I learned to keep my mouth shut. If I protested or complained, I got the back of my head smacked, or a cackling

Stack 'em high. *(Image Dan221 from the collection of the German Settlement History Inc., Ogema, WI)*

chorus of "chicka-dee-dee-dee" from the loggers doing their best imitation of the call of the tiny black and gray bird that was my namesake.

I remember those days in the same way I think about this goddamn war—dark. Feeling sorry for myself and a sense of despair. I was emotionally numb from the events that landed me in that camp. It is the same numbness the GIs develop seeing the shit we've seen the last two-and-a-half years.

My mother died from influenza on the ship coming from Amsterdam. Hundreds of people on board got sick, but only some died. It didn't seem fair. She was younger and stronger than a lot of the people who were sick but recovered. Why her?

We were moving to Chicago from Frankfort to live with my uncle Friedrick Schmidt, my mother's older brother. All I knew about him I learned from family stories, a few old photographs, and two letters. I knew he was married, had three or four children, and was developing a business. Evidently, he would buy grain from farmers then sell and deliver it to small breweries and bakeries. Mother told me I could tend his horses when we arrived. I loved animals, especially horses. While apprehensive about moving to America, the notion of being around the animals gave me something to look forward to.

My Uncle Friedrick came to America with my grandparents a few years before the First World War broke out. My mother told me her father predicted that the war would come and he didn't want any part of it. He had fought in the Franco-Prussian War. Even though that was barely a skirmish, my grandfather didn't want his sons drafted.

So in 1897, when he was forty-four, my grandfather sold everything and moved with his wife and three sons to America. Two of his daughters, including my mother, begged to stay in Germany and live with their grandmother. Her parents eventually acquiesced. My mother was fourteen and her sister Rose was seventeen. They were both still in school and working with a neighbor as seamstresses. My mother told me she just simply couldn't imagine leaving her friends and her life in Germany, even if it meant staying behind while her parents and brothers immigrated. They promised to visit and write often.

My mother never saw her family again. But they wrote. Mother showed me their letters—each one encouraged her to join them, even the letters telling her of my grandparent's deaths. My grandfather died first, at fifty-four, according to my uncle, succumbing to black lung disease from thirty years in the coal mines near Köln. My grandmother died just one year later in a tuberculosis sanitarium at age fifty.

3

In 1915 when I was three years old, my father was drafted into the German army. When he came home on leave, he didn't say much about what the trenches were like. I only remember him being home twice before he was killed. My mother and I received a telegram from the army informing us that father died at a makeshift hospital from shrapnel wounds just three days after returning to his unit following his last furlough. The only story my father told me about the war was when he jumped into a bomb crater when an artillery barrage started. Mustard gas from the previous shelling had settled in depressions and lingered there. He tried to make light of it, telling us how lucky he was to jump in and stay near the upper lip of the hole. He only suffered some burns to his mouth, throat, and ankles. Every other soldier that took cover there died. He said he didn't realize he had breathed in any gas, but he felt the burning on his ankles. He knew from experience not to give in to the overwhelming urge to scratch the itching, burning sensation caused by the gas exposure. He had seen guys literally scratch themselves to death trying desperately to relieve the itching. The scratching only opened more abrasions for the gas to enter.

Except for that story and a few comments here and there, he didn't want to talk about it. When home, he only wanted to hear about the home-front, the family, talk of plans for after the war, the garden, almost anything but the war. But his raspy voice from the gas burns, sullenness, and forced smiles, even as a kid I knew he was hiding a lot.

When the news came later that month that my father had been killed, it devastated Mother. She was never the same again. We had seen the officers come to other homes, read the casualty list posted at the telegraph station and churches, and heard from our neighbors who were informed of the deaths of their husbands or sons. Mother was an empathetic woman, but there was visible relief in her face that it was another family receiving the news of a death and not her.

The first word of my father was from a neighbor who had visited the telegraph station and had seen my father's name on the latest casualty list. We hoped that he was just wounded. Maybe it was just another whiff of gas. But the next day a chaplain and sergeant major confirmed our worst fear. I'll never forget the date—August 24, 1918. I heard my mother gasp when she saw the men walking up our steps. She couldn't look at them when we opened the door. Crying, she took their letter and listened to their words but I don't think she heard a word they said. She was obliviously still standing in the open doorway long after the men had left. She finally acknowledged me hugging her leg and knelt to hug me. I was crying, too, mostly because she was. Our neighbors came by to offer support and condolences, and to provide whatever help they could. People had to say something, but the words didn't matter.

His death was a lot harder on my mother. I loved him sure, but he had been gone for most of three years, nearly half my life at that point. When he was away I relied entirely on my mother. She changed when he died. Before, she would smile and sing while she cooked or baked. But even months after Father died the dark circles under her eyes made her look old, her smiles were fleeting, and I never heard her sing again.

When the war ended, Mother and I struggled to get by. Food and fuel were rationed if they were available at all. Everything became outrageously expensive. Inflation soared and paper money lost its value. First, it was twenty Deutschmarks for a loaf of bread, then hundreds, and finally thousands.

My mother bartered her sewing in exchange for whatever she could get. She seemed to be sewing all the time. Some of the boys came back after being gone for three or four years and were much taller, most were skinnier. I remember the butcher's son coming over to be fitted. He had lost an arm and most of his right shoulder. I knew it was impolite to stare, but I had never seen a disfigurement like that. He wanted my mother to fit his shirts and jacket with a pad to compensate. When he left, I remember my mother saying how lucky we were to do work for the butcher because he would pay with sausages.

Women I didn't know came by for alterations. They would stand on a small wooden box in front of a floor-length mirror while my mother pinned the fabric. Some chatted on about how they wanted something nice to wear to look their best now that their men were back. My mother, with pins in her mouth just nodded while they talked, but I could tell the talk about their men coming home was painful for her to hear. Women told her she was an artist, making seemingly new clothes appear from a pile of rags and old uniforms they brought in.

My parents kept a small hoard of gold and silver coins. Father accumulated much of this savings working as a carpenter before he was drafted. As the war approached, work was plentiful, particularly building munitions wagons for the army. Father had been working sixteen-hour days for several months and was being paid twice his usual wage. Manpower was in short supply once the draft was implemented, and having a family he was initially deferred from the draft. He converted the paper money he was paid into silver and gold coins. He was a realist. I remember him telling Mother that they had to consider what would happen if Germany lost the war and paper money would have little value. Both happened.

His hard work, pragmatism, and common sense paid off for Mother and me even after he was gone. Following the war there was the soaring inflation, but also food riots and lawlessness. Mother was concerned and began to seriously consider opportunities for us to make a new life elsewhere.

Mother finally lost hope that our life in Germany would improve. In September of 1920 she decided we should use our savings to purchase train tickets to Amsterdam and passage from there on a freighter to America.

Soon after the war started, but before the U.S. entered, we got a letter from her brother Friedrick urging us to join him in Chicago. After losing Father and the struggles after the war, Mother thought it would be best to start a new life with her brother and his family. She wrote them a letter about her plan to take them up on their offer, and we prepared to move to America. My extraordinary year of transformation—my year as a Chickadee—was about to begin.

When we were getting ready to leave, neighbors stopped over to say their goodbyes. I think many of them were envious. We left for the train station with five suitcases made of cardboard and gunny sacks; everything else we sold or gave away. Once the train reached the countryside, I couldn't believe the devastation. Mile after mile of eviscerated buildings, rubble, and fields pockmarked with shell holes, abandoned equipment, and trenches, just like it looks now that I'm back. I can only imagine how tranquil and scenic these rolling hills, farms, and small hamlets appeared during the twenty-year period between the wars.

4

My mother had difficulty finding tickets for passage, but after some searching was able to buy space on a freighter. We were packed in with a few doughboys and nearly twelve hundred émigrés from everywhere. Germans, Austrians, Ukrainians, Italians, Slavs, you name it, all heading to America. It was an odd blend. Some were conquerors, others the vanquished. The rich passengers were in berths, the rest of us huddled on deck. There was informal self-segregating of the passengers by nationality but little tension.

The trip started off well. There was a prevailing optimism and sense of camaraderie even among those who just a few months before were at war with each other. People were generally good-natured and hospitable despite the fact that it was crowded. Everything smelled of wet wool and of people unable to bathe. For most of my life to that point, we had to do without and I grew accustomed to working hard, and seeing suffering. But my mother insulated me from the harshness, and for me the boat trip was like a vacation, an adventure.

I made friends with children my age. Mother was relaxed and at ease for the first time since I could remember. Although leaving Germany and home was difficult, we were also leaving terrible memories, hardships, and uncertainties. Mother told me that the hardest part was making the decision to leave. Having made the decision, she said it was like a heavy veil had been lifted and our future was finally becoming clearer and brighter.

The trip across the Atlantic went to hell in a hand-basket in a hurry. The first case of the flu developed on board four days after embarking. Within a week, there were scores of cases. No medical facilities were available on the freighter. All the crew could do was try to keep the sick as comfortable as possible. Most victims were isolated on deck, bundled up and clutching their belongings. Every morning deck hands would gather the dead. At first the families were gathered, a few words said, and the deceased were dropped over the side of the ship from an inclined plank. Within a few days, the dead and sometimes dying were simply tossed overboard at the closest point to the victim. The ship's crew initially attempted to retain the valuables and identification papers of victims to return to their families. Later, as the death toll and the fear of contamination mounted, the crew gathered anything near the deceased and was interred at sea with the body.

I was one of the first to become ill. I remember the persistent and painful coughing, chills, and aches. These symptoms lasted a few days, and I recovered in a week. I didn't get the extreme fever or choking pneumonia that others like my mother did. She was dead within three days of the onset of symptoms. It's still painful to remember her wheezing and the bloody foam at the corners of her mouth as she struggled to breathe. About ten percent of the passengers and crew died during passage, two out of three got the flu.

The day before she died, my mother gave me the handful of silver and gold coins, a wad of Deutschmarks, the family bible, my birth certificate, father's letters, and the letter from Uncle Friedrick with instructions on how to contact him. She made me promise I would live with my uncle's family. The last thing she gave me before she succumbed was her wedding ring.

Combined with the residual weakness and nausea from my own bout with the flu and the feeling of utter despair following my mother's death, I couldn't eat or sleep. I huddled in a sheltered corner of the deck. That's how I celebrated my eighth birthday in October 1920. Frankly I wanted to die. I wandered to the railing of the ship and peered down into the slate gray froth and waves rushing below. I thought about my favorite times with her. It was when she read to me. It didn't matter what she was reading. It was feeling her warmth and hearing her voice and laughter that made that closeness special. I leaned farther over the railing, both feet gradually lifting off the deck. I was ready to just roll over the rail and drown in the sea.

I don't know what made me drop back onto the deck. But once the moment passed I didn't get that feeling again. The rest of the voyage was a blur until the day we were within sight of New York. I overheard the other passengers talking about the port officials refusing to let our freighter dock because of the flu outbreak. For several hours we sailed in a circle while the authorities tried to sort things out. A horn blast announced that we were cleared for entry into the port. From what I was able to understand, some diplomat on board evidently pulled some strings, which led the authorities to allow all passengers to disembark to a TB asylum on Long Island for a thirty-day quarantine.

The ship ported. I'm not sure where but I could see the Statue of Liberty from the pier. We were all ushered into a holding area on shore. Police wore white masks covering their nose and mouth, formed us into single-file columns, and marched us a half-mile up the coast to an asylum. Since I no longer had symptoms I was herded into a long narrow corridor on the first floor with others who also were not ill. It was nice to sleep in a bed again instead of on the ship's deck. Those with the flu either died or recovered. There were few new cases and within two weeks the quarantine was lifted for most of us.

5

Those of us discharged from the asylum were marched back to the pier where we landed and were shuttled by ferry the short distance to Ellis Island. Once there we were lined up for processing.

I stood with the others in line for three hours, winding slowly through a corridor. I was finally next, and face-to-face with a seated official. He asked me my name and I must have mumbled my reply because he loudly repeated his question in perfect German.

"What is your name?!"

"Wilhelm Heinlein."

"Who are you with?"

"I am traveling alone."

"Either you're with family or it's off to an orphanage," he said and reached for a different form.

That slapped me to attention. If I didn't successfully pass this point I wouldn't be able to find my Uncle Friedrick. That was my promise to my mother and my only real hope of getting some stability and security back into my life.

I thought quickly and lied a little, telling him, "I am meeting my uncle here in New York." I dug out the letter from my bag and handed it to him. "My uncle is meeting me and will be taking me to Chicago to live with him."

After reading the letter, the official began filling in the original form he had in front of him. "Do you have any papers?" I pulled out my passage papers and he copied some of the information.

"What is your birth date?"

"October 2, 1912."

"Do you have any money?"

I produced two crumpled 10,000 Deutschmark bills. I hoped the large numbers would be impressive.

"These are worthless," he said.

Then I remembered mother telling me that the gold and silver coins were more valuable even though their face value was only a fraction of the paper money. I opened the small pouch they were in for the official to see.

"How are you going to reach your uncle?"

"He is waiting for me."

"Where?"

"Here in New York."

"But *where*?!"

I dutifully repeated the instructions mother had given, embellishing a bit to better meet the circumstances.

"I'm to check into an inn and wire my uncle in Chicago to tell him where I am. The money I have should be enough for the room, food, and wire. If not, he will simply pay whatever is owed when he gets here," I said. Even as I spoke I thought it sounded feeble.

To my amazement and relief, that plan was sufficient and he proceeded with my processing without further inquiry. He wrote some more, produced three ink stamps, pounded them onto the paperwork, and handed two papers from the stack to me. He stood, grabbed my chin and wrote the letters "DP" in grease pencil on my forehead.

"Go to your left," he instructed.

I followed others toward a sign reading "Displaced Persons." There was one more stop. A lady in a gray uniform took my papers, handed me a packaged lunch, and pointed to a ferryboat I was to board for a ride back across the harbor to the port of New York. On October 20, 1920, I became an American.

Once seated on the ferry, I dug into the lunch box. A cheese sandwich that I devoured in four bites and an apple I saved for later. Listening to the other passengers and crew on the ferry, I was happy my mother insisted that we practice speaking English before we left Germany. And I got lucky that day and ran into Deiter. Great guy. Took me under his wing and taught me enough English to get by.

6

Deiter Pzybylski was seated next to me. He was talking a mile a minute, so excited he could hardly sit still. His long disheveled sandy blonde hair danced as he spoke. He didn't seem to care to whom he spoke or whether they listened. He was on his way to become a lumberjack in Bayfield, Wisconsin. Half listening, I gathered that his older brother had come to America to find work, joined a group of Poles headed to Wisconsin, and had been hired by a lumber company. Deiter spoke in the direction of an old man sitting across from us. The old man did his best to ignore him, but Deiter continued undeterred. His brother had a lot of work. The war effort created a huge demand for lumber. Now the demand was for new homes and apartments needed by the soldiers returning from Europe and the flood of immigrants. They just couldn't cut enough trees. He had to go to Chicago and then catch the train north.

At the mention of Chicago, I became interested. That's where my uncle was.

"What do you know about Chicago? That's where I'm going, too," I interrupted.

He smiled at me as though grateful to have someone show an interest, even if it was just a little German kid.

"Not much," he said. "There're lots of Poles there though."

We introduced ourselves and chatted a little in German. Deiter spoke English pretty well. Whenever he inadvertently spoke in Polish, he would stop and begin again in English.

19

We both wanted to practice speaking English and my English wasn't that good, but we also wanted to have a conversation. "Where are you staying tonight?" I asked.

"Don't know for sure, but it shouldn't be too hard to find someplace in a city this big."

I told Deiter that maybe I would stay at the same place, and we could end up on the same train to Chicago after I contacted my uncle. Deiter said that would be fine with him. On shore I had trouble keeping up with him. He walked quickly and with the excitement of a man eager to begin a new chapter in his life. As we left the wharf in search of a bowery flophouse, we passed a group of men. They stood on the wood walkway leading to the street above the wharf. We had to walk around them. They didn't say or do anything but tried to make eye contact with Deiter. He ignored them, but I couldn't. They looked menacing and I wasn't sure why, but they scared the hell out of me.

Within a couple of blocks Deiter found an inn that suited him and we entered. The lobby was a menagerie of sailors, doughboys, émigrés, and dock workers—but not one woman or anyone near my age. It was cheap, and they had a room available—one room. Deiter paid for the room we both would share. In the room I offered Deiter money for my half of the cost. Deiter declined and told me the room would cost the same whether he stayed there alone or not, so I shouldn't worry about it. I got the feeling that wasn't entirely true.

The room was eight by ten feet with a bed, chair, rickety night table, and a spittoon. A single electric light bulb attached to the end of an exposed cord dangled from the center of the ceiling. The two windows in the room were side by side on the same wall. The mattress smelled moldy and the table, chair, and windowsills were covered with a coat of coal dust. It was a dump, but I was just happy to have a place to go that first night in New York and someone to help me. I don't know what I would've done without Deiter.

I can still picture him in that room, sitting in the lone chair tilted backward until it was on two legs and rested against the wall, his feet on the bed next to me. We talked into the night, or rather Deiter talked. His excitement was becoming infectious. I realized that I, too, was on a life-changing and hopefully a life-improving adventure. Until that point, I hadn't taken time to think much about my uncle. As I half listened to Deiter, I wondered what my uncle was like. What kind of house he had? What would Chicago be like? I tried to imagine my uncle's family. Deiter continued to talk about Deiter.

He was the youngest of three brothers and fifteen when the war started. Too young for the draft, he filled in on a railroad crew that laid new track and repaired tracks and bridges damaged by shelling. Initially Deiter was used only when local work required a larger crew, but as the war progressed there was a manpower shortage. Eventually, Deiter became a specialist who would climb damaged rail bridges to remove debris, stabilize unsafe areas, and enable the main crew to begin reconstruction. I got the impression that Deiter liked it and was probably good at it. I would have been terrified to climb among tangled girders a hundred or more feet above a gorge, carrying a four-foot iron pry bar. Deiter joked that it was just like when he played tag on the beams in the family's barn with this brothers—a favorite activity for the boys after chores were done. If not tag, Deiter and his brothers engaged in impromptu physical dares, bets, and challenges. Some sounded dangerous to me. After dark they ate a late supper and played chess until bed. Deiter asked me what I liked to do best. After hearing what he did, I just shrugged my shoulders and decided not to share with him that my favorite pastime was having my mother read to me.

His life was so much more interesting than mine and he was only ten years older than I was. I decided then that I was going to be like Deiter.

When not working on the railroad crew, Deiter stayed at home to help with the family farm. The oldest brother, Michael, was drafted before the war to play chess as a representative of the Russian army. But when the war started, he was able to steal his way out of England and go to America. Their middle brother, Jan, remained home with Deiter until the war started. Jan was drafted but did not report. Instead he joined the resistance fighting both the Germans and Russians as the front moved east, then west and back again, ravaging Poland. Jan was killed in a skirmish with Russian soldiers.

Eventually we both drifted to sleep, Deiter in the chair, me diagonal on the bed.

The next morning before we set out to find a telegraph station we had breakfast. I ate the apple I had been saving from the boxed lunch for breakfast. Deiter produced a piece of cheese and hard salami from his coat pocket and offered me some. I declined because I didn't want to be obligated to share my apple.

When we finished eating we left the room and walked through the empty lobby. It smelled of beer, men, and mold. New York was much bigger than Frankfort or any city I had seen from the train to Amsterdam. Deiter compared it unfavorably to Warsaw before the war. With directions from a passerby we found a Wells Fargo telegraph station. I had drafted a letter in my mind for my uncle. I intended to tell him about the death of my parents, the voyage here, Deiter, where I was staying, and then ask a host of questions. Deiter went first.

He hadn't seen his brother in three years since the first stop of his brother's army chess tournament series. From what Deiter said the night before, he had only heard from his brother three or four times since and nothing in the last two years. Despite all he had to say, his message read simply, "Father, Mother, Jan dead. Arr. Hayward by train 28th. Leave directions. Deiter."

It was now my turn. The telegraph agent and Deiter chuckled when I began to dictate my wire. The agent stopped me before I finished. He informed me that each letter of each word increased the price and that unless I was "a Rockefeller" I may want to abbreviate somewhat. With

Deiter's help my new message read, "In NY, E'side Boarding House 3rd St. Mother died in route. Here alone. Hope to stay with you. Pls Reply. W. Heinlein."

We returned two days later. Deiter had received a telegram reading simply "Heard about Jan, not Mom and Dad. Will pick you up in Hayward. Mike." I received nothing. If I was to take advantage of the opportunity to travel with Deiter, he needed to know something today. We returned to the telegraph office later that afternoon. By then my message had been returned without a reply. My message couldn't be delivered. Friedrick's family had moved. The news was a crushing blow. What the hell was I going to do? Before I could fully comprehend my situation or consider my next move, Deiter said, "Hey, why not come with me? I've always wanted a little brother."

In the absence of any other option, Deiter's offer seemed pretty good and I was happy to accept. We planned to leave the next morning. That evening Deiter again talked well into the night. He paused periodically to ask to me a question related to his story, probably to see if I was still awake. I was. I enjoyed listening to him.

It seemed odd to me when Deiter stopped suddenly in mid-sentence. He was listening and his eyes were riveted to the shadows coming through the gap at the bottom of the door to our room. At that instant the door burst open and two men rushed in. The first man to enter had used his shoulder to break the feeble latch on our door and his momentum carried him nearly onto my lap. He grabbed me by my hair with his left hand, cast me toward the corner of the room and stabbed at me with the knife in his right hand. The blade cut through my jacket and shirt and nicked my rib. I tumbled into the corner of the room.

The second man lurched at Deiter with a knife. Deiter rolled off the bed and pulled a knife from his boot all in one motion and stood facing the thug as he lunged at Deiter. Turning his body sideways to the thrust, Deiter was able to elude the blade. He jumped forward parallel to the outstretched arm of the assailant. In a sweeping motion with his knife hand riding over the man's arm, Deiter cut a deep gash across the entire right side of the man's neck. Without looking back, Deiter sprang at the other man who was busy emptying out my bag onto the bed. The man was oblivious to Deiter, probably assuming he was being dispatched by his partner. I huddled in the corner frozen in terror. From there I saw the surprised expression on the man's face as he looked up at the same instant Deiter plunged his knife into the center of the man's belly. Deiter used such force that it looked as though the entire blade and half of the handle were buried in the man's gut. With a second motion Deiter violently lifted the blade straight up until it was stopped by the bottom of the man's sternum. The man didn't fall; instead he appeared to sit down cross-legged, like you might at a campfire. Deiter's attention went back to the man with the neck wound. He was leaning against the wall opposite from where I sat. Both of the man's hands clutched his neck and blood pulsed through his fingers. Deiter began to walk back toward him, but the man listed to his left and fell hard to the floor before Deiter reached him. Someone else evidently was at our open door. I couldn't see him from my corner. But when Deiter turned to face the door, I heard the sound of running footsteps disappear down the hallway.

The look in Deiter's eyes, his blood soaked shirt, and knife in hand likely discouraged the visitor from any involvement he had in mind. Deiter closed the door as far as he could. It was too damaged to shut completely but it would prevent passersby from looking into the room. He took off his bloody shirt and said, "We have to get the hell out of here."

Using the shirt, he wiped his hand and then pulled it over the blade of his knife before returning it to his boot. Rolling the shirt into a ball, he tucked it in his bag and put on his peacoat.

"Come on Will, let's go before their friends get here. These are two of the men from that group we passed on the dock."

It wasn't until Deiter grabbed the front of my jacket and

pulled me to my feet that I was able to move. He pushed my bag into my chest and threw his on the floor by the window.

We were on the second floor. If it wasn't for me I think Deiter would already have jumped from the window and escaped down the alley. Instead he opened the window and stuck his head out. He quickly pulled his head back in, stepped to his right and opened the second window.

"Let's go! Use the downspout," he said.

Tossing both bags out the window, he waited an instant for me to climb out. When I didn't respond quickly enough he lifted me onto the windowsill and pushed me out. I had to grab the six-inch tile pipe running from the roof to the ground or I would have fallen.

"Climb down!" he shouted, losing patience.

I was able to shinny down a few feet before losing my grip and falling hard to the ground. Looking up I saw Deiter clutch the pipe with his left hand and place his left foot on a toehold created by a bent tin strap used to hold the pipe against the wall. Grabbing the pipe with his right hand he was able to shift his weight from the ledge and support himself with his grip and the toehold while he pulled his right foot from the window ledge and placed it firmly against the pipe. Applying pressure on the pipe with the side of his feet and hands he slid effortlessly to the ground.

Moving quickly, Deiter picked up both bags, thrust mine at me and started down the alley. I gathered my wits and ran after him.

"Don't run!" he snapped, trying to whisper a shout. "Walk at my pace next to me."

As we walked briskly for two blocks I could hear shouts and the sound of running boots on the cobblestone street leading back toward the boarding house. When we turned a corner, Deiter said, "Now run!"

We ran some distance, probably ten or twelve blocks before Deiter pointed to a dark alley. There we hunkered down in the shadows next to a wooden loading dock protruding from a warehouse.

It had been midnight when the intruders broke into our room. After that I have no recollection of time. Deiter said we should stay there for the night and then make our way to the train station first thing in the morning. About an hour after we hid, we watched as three men walked by the alley. They stopped and looked in. Each explored the shadows with their eyes looking for something, probably us. After taking a few steps into the alley, they turned in unison and left.

I wanted to show Deiter the cut on my side. It was starting to throb and my shirt felt damp by the wound. But I must have fallen asleep, because the next thing I remember is seeing Deiter crouched over a muddy puddle rinsing out his shirt. It was dawn.

"It's my best shirt." He lifted it from the puddle, wrung it out, shook it and held it up to take a look at his work. "Not bad!"

The crimson blotches were gone but the entire shirt was now pink. "I'll do a better job later." He laid the damp shirt on the landing to dry and asked me if I was okay.

I didn't want to show Deiter how frightened I was. But thinking that I may have been severely wounded, I opted to let the evidence speak for itself. I raised my shirt to expose the gash on my side. He bent down to get a good look and quickly proclaimed, "Good, neither of us got hurt." Although disagreeing with his diagnosis, I kept quiet.

Before heading to the train station Deiter cautioned me that the men he killed belonged to a gang and their friends would be looking for us. We needed to remain on alert. I kept thinking about the events of that night and of Deiter. How could he be so capable and so confident, and seem to know exactly what to do? I really admired Deiter. But I was ashamed of myself for cowering in the corner. I asked him how he was able to overtake two men with knives by himself. He shrugged his shoulders, "They were drunk."

We began our walk to the rail station to buy tickets on the next available train to Chicago. Deiter seemed tense. He was uncharacteristically silent. His eyes were in constant motion, scanning the people on the street. I looked up at Deiter to ask him a question. His eyes were riveted on a man standing on the corner ahead. "What's the matter?" He didn't answer.

We passed the man without incident and I felt relieved until Deiter whispered, "He's following us."

We arrived at the station and bought two tickets on the nine-fifteen train. There were two runs daily from New York to Chicago, the nine-fifteen and the three-ten. We were fortunate that there was space available and would only have to wait about an hour. Deiter found a bench for us in the middle of the most crowded section of the station. He passed several empty benches farther from the trains, where I would have preferred to sit. He sat facing a window looking out onto the street leading to the station entry.

"Who was following us?"

"He's the third guy. He came to our door last night but left for help. They're looking for us."

That was the man I couldn't see but heard running down the hall. He probably went to round up his friends. They were likely the men we heard running back to the boarding house and who we saw looking into the alley. Now he knew right where we were. As we sat at the station watching the clock's agonizingly slow march toward nine-fifteen, Deiter said he thought the gang figured the two of us were an easy mark when they saw us get off the ferry. One of them probably followed us to see where we'd spend the night so they could come back later and steal our belongings. Deiter speculated that the gang probably targeted immigrants— easy prey. Immigrants were in unfamiliar surroundings, and had more money on them the minute they stepped off the boat than they would after they had been in the city for a while. But an eighteen-year-old with a kid probably appeared particularly vulnerable. The man who followed us reappeared on the street outside the station, along with six others. Deiter was motionless. I thought we were trapped and just couldn't sit still.

27

A train whistle blew in the distance. A moment later it blew again, closer this time. The gang moved toward the station. As they entered, the nine-fifteen arrived. It was coming from Boston scheduled to arrive at nine o'clock to allow enough time for passengers to New York to get off and those going to Chicago to board. The timing couldn't have been better. Passengers leaving the train momentarily merged with those moving forward preparing to board. This created a large crowd that Deiter led me through, taking advantage of the commotion.

A uniformed conductor punched a hole in each of our tickets when it was our turn to board. Deiter headed for two seats on the opposite side of the train from the station. We watched as the gang split up and pushed through the crowd in search of us.

The doors were pulled closed by the conductor. A loud burst of steam signaled our departure and the train lurched forward. As it began moving, Deiter jumped to an empty seat across the aisle facing the station. He waved frantically until he got the attention of one of the thugs and quickly raised his bent left arm stopping it with his right hand, while muttering in Polish, "Up yours, boys."

Some of the more refined passengers scowled and shook their heads at Deiter. I didn't disapprove. I wanted to be just like him.

7

From the first day I met Deiter he was eager to talk about his plans, Poland, politics, but most of all his family. He loved conversation, particularly his, and he chatted on during much of the long train ride from New York. He might have found it therapeutic. For me it was an education and a source of entertainment.

Deiter stopped talking to watch the Pennsylvania scenery pass by, and dozed off. His voice was replaced by the gentle rocking of the car and metronomic clicking of the wheels on the track. The sound and motion were comforting, like being rocked by my mother, and reminded me of the train ride we took at the beginning of my journey. The landscape that passed by my window now was like an idealized, fairytale version of the Germany I left, littered with burned cities, skeletal homes and barns, and pockmarked fields. I closed my eyes, too.

I awoke to Deiter's familiar voice. He pointed me toward a newspaper being read by another passenger. The headline, "Bolsheviks Defeat White Army," served as the stimulus for Deiter's next topic, the Russians.

Most Poles hated the Russians. Deiter said that for the better part of a century Poland had been part of Russia. The Poles were fiercely independent and didn't do well under Russian control. They rebelled and resisted, which brought retaliation and harsher rule, further enflaming the anti-Russian sentiments. His brother Jan's anti-Russian sentiments were the strongest of the boys. When the war started, Jan joined the resistance. A week or two later he was drafted in absentia into the Russian army. Deiter's family didn't realize how much danger Jan's actions had put them in.

Deiter and Michael had been more philosophical. They resented Russian rule but understood Russia's interest in having a buffer zone between itself and the rest of Europe. For them, Russian rule was unfortunate but tolerable. That changed when Deiter saw his parents shot by a young Russian officer. When the Russians came to their house, Deiter had been clearing rocks that heaved to the surface after the winter frost. He piled the rocks onto a hedgerow at the far end of an unplowed field across the road from his house. His father had intended to plant barley there in a week. The Russians had suspected that there were Polish resistance fighters hiding in his family's barn. An informant must have told the officer that Deiter's parents aided the resistance. Confronted by the officer, his father denied it. The officer shot him point blank in the face. Deiter's mother screamed and lunged at the Russian.

When he heard the first shot, Deiter laid down next to the hedgerow. Unsure of the origin of the shot he peeked above the rocks. He saw his father on the ground, and then watched as the Russian shot his mother twice in the chest. He fought the compulsion to run to their aid, but instead stayed hidden. The Russians set his family's barn on fire. The four Polish nationals in the barn ran out. Two were shot dead. The two captured fighters were interrogated then bayoneted. The Russians then ransacked and burned the house.

With that, Deiter said he immediately set out to join the resistance, hoping to find his brother Jan's group. The family had heard nothing directly from Jan for over a year, but the men they hid in their barn knew him and said he was alive and well. The greatest danger to the resistance was informants—Ukrainians living in Poland, or fellow Poles. Informants and their families were scorned by their neighbors, but for some the special favors and awards paid by the Russians were too tempting.

Deiter wanted revenge against informants and the Russians. On his second night as a resistance aspirant, he sought out Russians and headed toward the sound of distant gunfire. He selected a nearby grove of trees that looked like a good place for him to spend the night. There he found a group of dead Russian soldiers. Deiter said it looked like the Russians had been dead for at least a couple of days, and that a single round of artillery had killed the soldiers. Being a single round and not part of a prolonged barrage made Deiter believe it was likely off-target friendly fire.

Deiter said he was lucky to find those dead troops. They had food and weapons, both of which he desperately needed if he was going to last more than a week on his own. Armed, he would be able to kill Russians, could extort food or supplies if necessary, and he would have value to the resistance. Being the first one on the scene he had the opportunity to pick and choose whatever items he wanted from the undisturbed remains. With no one else in sight Deiter leisurely rifled the pockets and belongings of the dead. He was surprised at the horde of valuables most of the soldiers had. Goods probably pilfered from Polish homes, maybe even his. In addition to looting the homes of anyone suspected of sympathizing with the resistance, soldiers extorted protection payments from professionals, shop owners and Jews who either paid or were harassed or worse. Deiter emphasized the point that he thought fighting the Russians using supplies, money, and weapons stolen from Russians who had looted from his neighbors was payback.

Deiter said his first encounter with a resistance went very badly. He encountered a group in the hills a few miles from the dead Russian soldiers. He didn't trust anyone, nor did the resistance. This resulted in a standoff. The resistance leader couldn't convince Deiter to come out of hiding because Deiter insisted on knowing who they were first. Neither side wanted to exchange gunfire for fear of drawing the attention of the Russians. Deiter was not about to drop his weapon and simply walk out into the open as they demanded. They could easily be Ukrainian or German army deserters, a gang of bandits, or Russian regulars on a sortie to ferret out resistance. In the end Deiter crawled backward for about a quarter mile and then stealthily swung north and west to circle away from the group. He decided at that point it was too dangerous to try to join a resistance group unless he was introduced by someone he knew and trusted, like his brother Jan.

He knew Jan had joined a group with several school friends right after the German invasion in 1914. The eastern front shifted throughout Poland, with the resistance caught between the Russians on the east and Germans on the west. Ninety percent of resistance fighters were killed in skirmishes or captured and tortured after being identified by informants. Deiter understood their suspicious nature. Not having heard from Jan for many months, Deiter held out hope that the lack of contact was just a precaution to avoid any implication of the family or simply the result of difficulty communicating in a war zone; or maybe Jan heard that his parents were killed and their home burned. After all, the men they hid in their barn said they knew Jan and that as far as they knew he was well. While those men were killed, perhaps there were other resistance units in the area at the time their parents were killed. They would have heard about what happened and relayed the news to Jan.

8

While Deiter didn't come right out and say it, he seemed embarrassed that his experiences during the war included a lot more hiding than fighting. There were large blocks of time unaccounted for during Deiter's recitation. When I asked him to fill some of the time gaps he either obliged superficially or said he didn't remember. One episode however was an exception, and he was clearly pleased with himself when he described what happened.

Two weeks after his parents were killed, and thirty miles from his home, Deiter encountered a Russian patrol resting on the side of road having a smoke. He intended to wait for them to finish their break and get back on their way. After a safe interval he would cross the road to continue his journey. That was until one of the officers stood up to stretch. Deiter immediately recognized the blonde hair and unusually skinny frame. It was the Russian he saw from the barley field. It was the son-of-a-bitch that he watched shoot his parents, burn his farm, and kill the resistance fighters his family was hiding. Deiter said he would have allowed the convoy to pass because it was too big a target for him to take on by himself. But once he recognized the Russian, Deiter said he didn't care if he died or not, as long as he was able to kill that officer.

Deiter said he was too far away to get a good shot and needed to get closer quickly. Halfway between the edge of the forest where he was and the road stood a beech tree surrounded by high grass. Deiter said it would've taken too long to crawl that distance. As a child he often hunted wild pigs on the forested craggy hills near his home with his father and brothers. Approaching these wary animals was difficult. A common technique his father taught him was when they would spot a boar at a distance, to try to position a tree between you and the pig. With the tree blocking the boar's line of vision, you could then walk briskly but silently toward it. Once at the tree, you either try for a shot or move closer repeating the process.

Deiter said the officer stood and casually scanned the woods where Deiter was hiding. Deiter moved to his right to better position the tree between him and the officer's line of sight. Once lined up with the tree, he took off his backpack and bedroll and left them in the woods. In position, he noted where the other six soldiers were and the direction they were looking. One was posted at the front of the vehicles keeping a lookout down the road. The others were leaning against their motorcycles as they sat on the ground with their backs to Deiter.

Believing his chances were as good as they were going to get, Deiter stood, put his rifle parallel to his body to keep his profile as narrow as possible, and walked to the tree. Its two-and-a-half-foot diameter provided the concealment he needed. Once there, he crouched behind the tree and below the top of the grass, brought his rifle up and held it firmly against the tree for support, and took aim.

Deiter laughed when he told me that it was at that point he realized he still hadn't fired the Mosin-Nagant rifle he had taken from one of the dead Russians he found in the woods. Not knowing the accuracy or nuances of the sight, he just decided to aim for the center of the officer's chest. His plan was simple, shoot as many of the soldiers as possible and try to get back to the woods.

He said he lined up the vertical post on the end of the barrel of his rifle with the center of the V-shaped sight with his target and steadied his aim. The officer scanned the area and looked directly at Deiter. They made eye contact just as Deiter squeezed the trigger. His shot was high, missing the chest but hitting the officer just below the chin, entering the throat and exiting through the back of his neck.

Deiter said he pulled back behind the tree to bolt another round into the chamber. Gunfire erupted from the remaining Russians, but he was surprised that they were just shooting wildly into the woods. Evidently they didn't know where he was. So he just sat back against the tree and stayed still. After a minute or two, the Russians started their motorcycles, put the body of the dead officer in a sidecar, and sped off. Deiter said he peeked around the tree to see if he could get another shot off at the fleeing Russians. They were too far away so he just watched the motorcycles speed down the dirt road, the officer's dead body bouncing and bobbing in the sidecar like a marionette.

9

U p to that point Deiter said it had been relatively easy for him to survive in the woods and spend an occasional night in a barn. He rarely encountered the Russians and the weather had been mild. But as winter approached he knew that would be another story, and he was concerned. He would need to have a fire every night and he'd leave tracks in the snow leading right to his camp. It was never easy, but it would become even more difficult to steal chickens and other animals from nearby farms once they were sheltered in coops or barns for warmth. He needed to build a cache of food in preparation.

One evening while on a food-finding sortie, Deiter said he watched from a distance as a small Russian patrol walked up to a farmhouse. They rapped loudly on the door and entered. Deiter thought he might be able to get close enough to take a shot at the officer and then get away before the others could react. He changed his plan when he spotted what he described as the "provision mother lode"—piglets. Getting food was a priority. Easy to snatch and carry, one piglet could feed him for a week or more. The nine piglets in the litter were lying next to their four hundred pound mother. Deiter learned as a youngster how aggressive and dangerous sows can be. While playing tag with his brothers and neighbor boys at a nearby farm, he told me how he hopped over the fence of a sow's pen to escape being tagged. The sow, which appeared to be sleeping against the opposite side of the pen, charged at him, biting and shredding his boot as he scrambled to make his escape over the four-foot wood and wire fence. The sow left him with a three-inch gash on his ankle and heel. He still had the scar.

But Deiter said a piglet was worth the risk, even if the risk included a Russian patrol. As long as he could execute his plan quickly and quietly he would be safe. Approaching cautiously, he surveyed the situation looking for the easiest entry and exit point. The quickest and safest means would be to reach through the slats of the pen, grab the nearest piglet, dispatch it with his knife, and safely pull the carcass back through the slats. Although the piglets were too big to fit through the openings between the slats, if he broke off the bottom of one or two of the vertical boards of the pen the plan could work. Deiter broke off the bottom foot of a board adjacent to another already missing a piece. The piglets noisily moved to the opposite side of the pen. The sow remained where she had been, but her head was raised and she stared menacingly at Deiter. He was concerned that the commotion would draw the attention of the Russians and said he either needed to succeed now or come back another night. He said he decided to gather stones that he intended to toss at the piglets to frighten them into running around the pen, hoping to be able to snatch one as it ran by the opening. Deiter stood up and lobbed a stone in the piglets' direction. They scattered across the pen. One piglet tried to escape through the opening Deiter made earlier, and became momentarily stuck. The jagged edge of the broken board caught the back of the piglet as it tried to squeeze through the opening. It was just enough time for Deiter to run back and grab the pig by its ears and pull it through.

The commotion alerted the men in the farmhouse. Deiter said he tucked the squealing, kicking piglet firmly under his left arm, took hold of its front legs with his left hand, and started running back to the hedgerow he came from. He was surprised when a volley of bullets whizzed past him, followed by the lagging report of the gunshots, but reached the hedgerow before a second volley was fired.

It was dark and the soldiers were probably drinking and didn't give chase. Beyond the hedgerow Deiter ran across a hayfield and finally reached the safety of the woods where he slowed down to a jog. Deiter said he was exhilarated by his success, until the piglet threw its head back and bit him on the chin. Deiter said he had to use a flour sack he kept in his coat pocket to put over the pig's head to prevent it from doing any more damage. Once he reached the creek in an area he was more familiar with, Deiter said he slit the pig's throat, let it bleed out on the ground, and sat against a tree still breathing hard from exertion. He was bleeding, too, from the bite and pressed the wadded-up flour sack against the wound to stem the flow of blood. When the bleeding stopped and he felt rested, Deiter made his way back to camp.

About a week later he had eaten the last of the piglet, but was still putting disinfecting dabs of vodka from the last remaining flask he had taken from the dead Russians on the slow-to-heal gash on his chin. Deiter said he saved the last flask only because of its high barter value. He would have been able to trade it for a couple of pounds of cheese and bread loaves if he needed to.

A day or two later Deiter said he heard a distant sound like an army on the move. He worked his way toward the road nearest the sound, careful to stay several yards deep in the forest. The first of the troops crested over a hill a quarter mile away. They were Russians and were not marching in military formation. Heading east, they looked like they were retreating back to Russia. It took nearly three hours for the entire army to pass. Deiter watched a boy following the army and gathering any items lost or discarded by the marching mass. After the army was out of sight, Deiter approached. He said he was surprised that the boy, probably eleven or twelve years old, didn't appear to be frightened. Like Deiter's brothers and friends, a lot of farm boys admired the resistance, but they also knew they needed to remain cautious of strangers.

They greeted, sized each other up over small talk and began sharing news—timidly at first. Deiter said he quickly became confident that the boy was no threat. The boy must have felt the same way because their conversation warmed to a relatively free exchange. Deiter said he had heard that the Czar had been deposed earlier in the year. Revolution was underway in Russia and speculation was that Russia would exit the war. The boy told Deiter that his father had said the army was ordered to pull back to reinforce Riga, which along with the rest of Latvia, was being lost to the Germans. The Germans were advancing back through western Poland to fill the void left by the exiting Russians. There was talk of Russia trying to negotiate peace with Germany. The boy told Deiter that his father speculated that the Germans would be back in Pisz, about twenty miles from there, in a week or two. With a revolution underway at home, the Russian army was pulling back, leaving Poland to the advancing Germans.

Without prompting, the lad said he knew of a farm that an old woman had been left to run by herself. The woman's forty-five-year-old husband and two sons, Tanska and Henryk, were drafted into the Russian army. No one had received any word from them for a year. The woman, Mrs. Szeryng, was struggling to keep the farm going until the men returned. The boy suggested that Deiter could probably hide in her barn and she would never know. Deiter said he told the boy he was traveling in a different direction but thanked him for the suggestion. But the more Deiter thought about the boy's suggestion, the better it sounded. His options were to go to the Szeryng farm or another one he randomly selected. Deiter said he intentionally left going in a direction other than the one toward the old woman's farm, but once out of sight he turned north and began the five-mile walk cross-country toward the cluster of farms on the other side of the bridge spanning the Bug River. By habit, he waited until nightfall to cross the bridge. Just before setting out he noticed a faint glow under the bridge. He assumed it was a partisan fighter lighting a cigarette. Deiter didn't want another encounter with the resistance, but swimming and wading across a river the size of the Bug in November in northern Poland was stupid, and finding an unguarded available boat unlikely. He said he remembered that he had passed an old wheelbarrow leaning upright against a fence post a quarter-mile back. He thought maybe a lone man pushing a wheelbarrow of firewood wouldn't alarm the partisans and they would just let him pass without incident. He decided it was worth a try. If he was stopped, Deiter said he planned to tell them he was there to join the resistance, or use the information the boy had given to him earlier that day. Maybe they knew his brother Jan. Either way, Deiter said he was confident he had enough information to talk his way past them.

He gathered branches and sticks and loaded them onto the wheelbarrow. His intention was to look like any other farmer bringing home firewood on a cold November night. He covered his backpack and bedroll, slid his rifle into the branches so it was not visible but easily accessible, and started down the road toward the bridge, accompanied only by the squeak of a wobbling wheel. Just when he thought his ruse might be working, two men with rifles stepped out of the darkness. He assumed there were more, out of sight.

Deiter said one of the men called, "What the hell are you doing?"

"I am bringing firewood to the Szeryng farm. Mrs. Szeryng's son Henryk asked me right after he was drafted to look in on her if I could. It has taken some time but I was finally able to travel. I thought she may need some firewood," Deiter said he called back.

"You call that pile of sticks firewood?"

"It was an afterthought. She may have me sleep in the barn and arriving so late I thought I should have some wood on hand."

"What's your name?"

"Deiter Pzybylski."

"Do you know a Jan Pzybylski?"

"I have a brother Jan. Do you know where he is?"

"We do. He was killed west of the Masurian lakes by Russians. He took three of the scum with him."

They went on to tell Deiter that his brother had managed to stay alive for two years alternately fighting the Germans and the Russians. While seemingly futile, the resistance fighters were determined to fight occupiers of Poland and would do so until there was an independent Poland again. One of the men on the bridge was on that raid with Jan. He told Deiter that Jan's luck ran out in an ambush on a small Russian convoy. Jan was wounded in the groin and chest. Unable to move he was beyond hope of rescue. Jan knew the Russians would interrogate and then kill him. But Jan was ready with two grenades clutched to his chest. When the Russian soldiers were near enough, Jan pulled the pins of the grenades killing the Russians and himself. Based on what the men told him, Deiter figured it was about the time of Jan's death that the Russians killed his parents for their support of the resistance.

The conversation with the group then went to the Russian officer Deiter had shot months earlier. Deiter was told that the officer was the son of Russian General Sukeroff. The assassination led to fierce retaliation against the resistance, called off only after the orders to redeploy to Riga were received. Deiter said he could tell the men were impressed with his assassination of a high-ranking Russian officer, but they also told him that he was responsible for the increase in Russian counter-resistance efforts and the retaliation that followed.

There was a complicated relationship between the Poles and the resistance. Not all Poles supported the partisan fighters. Once the war started and Poles were drafted into the Russian army, resistance action aimed at killing Russian soldiers often resulted in killing drafted Polish men as well. Family members of draftees were hostile to those who tried to kill rank and file Russian army soldiers, so the resistance tried to focus on officers. That is just what Deiter had done.

It didn't take long for the men to embrace Deiter as a comrade. He said he was happy to finally join a resistance group. The men who knew Jan told Deiter what they could. Jan joined a group of former schoolmates staying near his home at first. His group later fled north when they heard that someone had informed the Russians of their location. By a stroke of luck they learned this from a young girl who, while playing in an alley, overheard a Ukrainian talking to soldiers. Jan's group barely slipped past the fifty Russian soldiers sent after them. They followed roughly the same route north Deiter had taken and joined forces with another partisan group. Jan had evidently made a name for himself within the resistance before his death.

Deiter said that the resistance leader took him to Mrs. Szeryng's door, made the introduction, and asked the woman if Deiter could stay in her barn for a while and help out around the farm. Deiter said she seemed reluctant, but said he could stay in the barn for the night and she would see how things went after that.

Deiter said the arrangement with Mrs. Szeryng turned out to be a perfect match. He performed all of the duties that Mrs. Szeryng had been neglecting on the farm. In return Deiter received a place to stay and meals in return. She welcomed the company and confided to Deiter that she felt better knowing the farm would be in a more presentable state when her men returned. At forty-four years old, Deiter said Mrs. Szeryng looked sixty-four. Evidently the hardships over the years had taken a toll. Mrs. Szeryng asked him to stay on until her men came home. Deiter agreed. He didn't have anywhere else to go, and Mrs. Szeryng reminded him of his mother. He was eager to help her.

Only her son Henryk returned. He had been released from a German prisoner of war camp after peace with Rus-

Deiter's refuge. *(Image 274 from the collection of the German Settlement History Inc., Ogema, WI)*

sia was declared. Deiter said Henryk was in terrible condition; his body was ravaged by dysentery and malnutrition from his time as a prisoner of war. Even then he was lucky. Germans didn't treat Russian prisoners well, but everyone knew German prisoners fared even worse with the Russians.

Henryk told them that his father had died in the same prison camp that he was in. All three Szeryng men were drafted at the same time and ended up in the same unit. During a campaign in 1916 near Brest-Litovsk, Henryk's younger brother was killed outright during the battle. The Russians were routed but mounted a feeble counterattack. It was poorly executed and resulted in the bulk of the army killed or captured, including the two remaining Szeryngs.

During the months following peace between Germany and Russia, Deiter said life for him, the Szeryngs, and most Poles slowly returned to normal. Germany focused their available manpower on the western front facing France, leaving the occupation of Polish territory, formerly part of Russia, up to the minimum number of troops necessary to quell rebellion and provide the western army with resources and reserves. Deiter said Germany used the Polish territory as a bargaining chip during truce talks and as a buffer against the increasing instability within Russia. Famine for the Szeryngs and most Poles was averted. The surviving decommissioned Polish soldiers returned to the farms and were able to get crops in the ground that spring. The previously rampant pillaging of food and livestock was reduced to sporadic raids by Germans, who were preoccupied fighting the Allies. Deiter said there was no reason to stir things up. There was little for a resistance fighter to do.

Deiter said he stayed with the Szeryng family for over a year after the armistice until Henryk had regained his strength and was able to work the farm again. The Szeryngs encouraged Deiter to stay on with them, but he said his mind was made up. He wanted to get out of Poland, immigrate to America and join his brother Michael. Deiter said he offered to pay the Szeryngs for their hospitality. They refused to accept anything, saying that they were indebted to Deiter as well. Deiter said he put fifty dollars worth of silver in their kitchen cupboard before he left. It was money he took from the dead Russians. While both he and the Russians owed the Szeryngs a lot more, Deiter said he needed the rest of his money to reach America.

10

After listening to Deiter's stories on the train ride from New York, I thought it ironic when he told me that just before the war his brother Michael had been an officer in the Russian army. Even though Deiter saved my life and made being a Chickadee and finding my family possible, it would be Michael who had the greatest influence on me.

Deiter described himself as the daredevil of the boys, while Michael was quiet, studious, and a voracious reader. Michael was nineteen when the war started in 1914. He was four years older than Deiter and two years older than Jan.

Michael was drafted into the Russian army before the war. The last time Deiter heard anything from his brother was a letter the family received in 1914 when Michael told them he deserted and was on his way to America. The letter, delivered by a Polish national returning from London, detailed Michael's plan to get a job at a lumber company. As far as Deiter knew, Michael was still working there. Deiter couldn't wait to join him and get caught up on Michael's life in America, and to share his own experiences during the war. He didn't look forward to telling Michael the circumstances surrounding their parents and brother's death.

Deiter and I arrived at the train station in Hayward, Wisconsin, on November 3, 1920. The six inches of new snow on the ground was crisscrossed by countless tracks of people, wagons, horses, and trucks—most leading to and from the rutted road adjacent to the station. The wind bit my

Almost there. *(Image BK022 from the collection of the German Settlement History Inc., Ogema, WI)*

uncovered ears the instant I stepped out of the train car onto the wooden platform beside the once red station. The sky was bisected with an ominous line of charcoal clouds, which ran diagonally to the horizon.

We each carried two bags that contained everything we owned. When we reached the end of the platform we dropped the bags at our feet. Deiter scanned the dozens of people standing and mingling outside the station and spotted Michael just as Michael saw him. I could see a clear family resemblance. Although Michael was taller, clean shaven with short black hair and handsome, compared to his round boyish-faced brother with a mop of hair. Both were skinny as saplings. They walked quickly toward each other. Awkwardly the brothers started to shake hands but simultaneously opted for a bear hug. At first there were no words. Then as if a starter's pistol had fired, they both began spewing a series of questions, news, and updates all without pause, and seemingly without taking a breath.

Michael held up his hand. They both stopped talking.

Michael asked Deiter to tell him first about their parents and Jan. They walked toward an old black truck with Seely Land and Lumber Company stenciled in yellow on the side. I followed. Deiter recounted the details of the deaths of their parents and brother as they walked. Michael had received a letter from a friend in London that a Pole with the same last name as Michael's was killed by the Russians two years earlier. His friend could not provide any corroborating evidence but felt the source was reliable. Deiter had rehearsed and refined his description of events to me on the train. His narrative to Michael was a concise description confirming what Michael's friend reported, as well as what the resistance fighters told Deiter about Jan. With the initial flurry of questions answered, Michael's attention briefly turned to me.

"Who's the deaf mute tagging along behind you?" Michael asked.

I think he was trying to engage me. I had only watched and listened, and probably hadn't made a peep since stepping off the train.

"I'm Will and I am not a deaf mute."

Deiter and Michael laughed at my indignant reply. Deiter told Michael of our chance meeting in New York and of my bad fortune.

"I was hoping we could get a stable-boy job or something like that at the lumber company for him," Deiter said.

Michael thought a moment. "You know, the last Chickadee up and left without a word a few weeks ago. He didn't even take all of his belongings. They will need to replace him before too long. Maybe that would work?"

Not having any idea what he was talking about I didn't answer. Deiter did.

"That would be great. See Will? You got yourself a job before you left the train station."

We embarked on the final leg of my journey to become a Chickadee—a bumpy forty-five minute ride from the train station to the logging camp. Michael and Deiter took turns telling the other something that had happened to them during the past four years. They were engrossed with each other's stories and largely ignored me. That was fine. I was too busy feeling sorry for myself and had no interest in trying to be sociable. Instead I listened and learned more about Deiter and a lot more about Michael.

"Deiter, I want to know everything. Tell me about Mother, Father, Jan, and I want to hear all about what you did during the war. Resistance fighter extraordinaire, I understand," Michael said.

"I'll have plenty of time once we're there, and I'm afraid after hearing my stories endlessly over the past six days, poor Will's head just might explode if I start all over again," Deiter said. I know he was joking but he was absolutely right.

"Before the letter you sent notifying us that you were going to come here, the last thing I heard was that you were leaving Kiev for a tournament in Moscow," Deiter said.

"Yeah, and from Moscow I went to England to play in chess tournaments there. That's where I was when the war started," Michael said.

Michael started talking about playing chess as kids. He must have been an exceptional player. From what I could gather, he and his brothers played chess virtually every evening. They used a chessboard and men they carved from scraps of cherry wood and maple. The winner kept playing while the loser was replaced by the third player. Michael rarely lost and if Jan beat Michael there was raucous celebrating. Deiter never beat Michael, at least not after Michael stopped letting him win, which he admitted doing occasionally when Deiter was small. Deiter must have been proud of Michael's gift for the game. He went on about how Michael was able to not only anticipate what would happen next, but could visualize the unfolding of the entire game after the first few moves. Michael corrected Deiter often when he exaggerated too much, but not then.

Deiter was very animated when he related how the boys learned to play chess from their father. Deiter hadn't talked about that in New York or on the train so I listened with greater interest. His father consistently beat Jan and him, but not Michael. Michael found the predictable patterns and tendencies in their father's game and invariably stayed a couple of moves ahead or set traps that their father just couldn't avoid. Deiter said Michael was the informal chess champion, not just of the family but of their community.

Michael took over telling the story from Deiter and began at the end of January, 1914. That must have been about the point where their lives began to diverge. During that winter there was a particularly bitter cold spell. The Russian army occupying Poland was sequestered to barracks and bored by inaction and peacetime. They were unaware that they would be at war within months. To help pass the time, Michael and other locals were invited to play chess at the Russian army post nearby. If nothing else, Michael shared the Russians' love for the game.

Michael beat all the players he faced most convincingly. Impressed, the commanding officer invited Michael to volunteer to join the army and become a member of the division's chess team. The officer told Michael he would have a chance to compete in chess tournaments all across Russia. Michael had no interest in enlisting in the Russian army and declined the offer. Two days later, soldiers arrived at the Pzybylski farm with Michael's conscription papers.

Even as a kid I couldn't believe someone would get drafted into the army to *play chess*. But like it or not, Michael was in the Russian army.

Michael said his father was incredulous and protested, "Poles fight against Russians! Not with them."

Michael said, "But, I will be fighting the Russians! Just using rooks and pawns."

Deiter laughed and nodded his head as he remembered the story.

Michael said he had no intention of doing any real fighting. While there were tensions, Europe was at peace. At that time, Michael thought he was just going to play some chess for the next six months until his commission expired, and resume his forestry studies at the College of Mining and Forestry, helping at home when he could.

Michael reminded Deiter that the Russian occupation had been a real benefit to him. He was one of the very few Polish farmers fortunate enough to be able to attend a technical college. He surmised that the Russians were desperate to modernize their industry and military after a humiliating naval defeat to the Japanese a few years earlier. They had begun recruiting boys from grade schools who excelled academically and were recommended by their headmasters as having mechanical aptitude. The technical schools were a good vehicle to develop workforce expertise needed to incorporate European technology and operate and repair the new machinery and weapons of war the Russians were importing. Michael was among the top candidates recommended from his school. After all of the sons of wealthy and well-connected Poles who remained loyal Czarists were placed, a handful of appointments remained to be filled by common Poles. Michael's had been one of them. Michael said that without that education he wouldn't have been able to get his job assessing timber, which paid a lot more than lumberjack pay.

Within a week of receiving his conscription papers, Michael traveled in Warsaw and played chess with army division champions from all across western Russia. Michael seemed to remember every one of his matches. In that tournament he said he won eighteen of twenty-four matches, drew on four, and lost twice. In March he was sent to Kiev, where he had similar success. At the end of April Michael was ordered to Moscow for the chess tournament held during the May Day celebration. Michael made it to the finals. He said he played Ivan Statenski, a twenty-eight-year-old three-time army champion and leading candidate for the new designation of Grand Master started that year by Czar Nicholas II.

In the first four games Michael said he was fortunate to have been able to salvage a draw in each game. Statenski was without a doubt the strongest player he had ever encountered. Facing defeat each time, Michael said he had to use every creative gambit and strategy he could muster. Michael laughed when he recalled how frustrated Statenski was that Michael was able to salvage draws. Michael and Statenski were the center of attention in what Michael described as the largest and grandest venue he had ever seen. He said it was a challenge to stay focused.

After four matches however, Michael said he had begun to detect Statenski's preferences. Deiter smiled and nodded when Michael said he had planned to set a trap for Statenski just like he had done so many times when he played Deiter, Jan, and his father.

Tournament players scored two points for a win and one point for a draw. The winner was the first player to reach five total points; with four draws the score was even. Statenski had white and opened with the same sequence he used in their first match. Michael said he assumed that Statenski felt that was his strongest game, since that was the opening he chose for their first game, and it worked well then. After three moves Michael said he was convinced Statenski intended to pursue the same strategy. I couldn't understand the specific moves of the game that Michael said he made, but Deiter seemed to. It sounded like he made the same moves he made in the first match with one exception. He delayed moving, I think it was his king bishop, and hoped it would not put Statenski on alert. Michael said that once he knew Statenski was committed Michael began a totally new strategy that was now possible because he could move his rook out to attack and then castled. Michael said those moves completely changed the board and rendered Statenski's plan ineffective.

The moves didn't yield any pieces but Michael said it gave him a two-move advantage, which was all he needed. After the twenty-ninth move, Statenski resigned. Michael said Statenski was trying to stay composed but looked stunned. Without a word, he turned his king on its side, stood up and exited the room.

Deiter said, "You won the May Day Tournament?"

Michael nodded, and described how the room had erupted in cheers and shouts, mostly coming from fellow Poles, and the Latvians and Estonians in attendance.

"The Russian army brass didn't seem too pleased to have a Pole win. One officer told me I insulted all Russians by winning." Laughing, Michael added, "That was the plan."

Michael went on to say that the May Day Tournament had been a warm-up for the Russian National Championship to be held in Moscow in July. It was clear to Michael that Statenski or some other Russian was supposed to win. A Muscovite is supposed to win that tournament.

In the third week in May, Michael said he got orders to pack. He had been assigned to a contingent of army chess players for a goodwill trip to England. The trip would take seven or eight weeks.

"By sending me to England, I would be conveniently unavailable to compete in the Russian Championship. I was still conscripted for three more months and the Russians intended to take full advantage of it. I arrived in London with the others in the middle of June, 1914. The itinerary included tournaments throughout England, Scotland, and Ireland. We were supposed to finish up in the third week of August."

Michael described being greeted in London by a small group of Polish expatriates living in Britain. One of them was a newspaper writer and author named Witold Whyse. Witold was going to follow the tournament and write about it. As a chess enthusiast and Pole, Witold told Michael he was looking forward to meeting him since hearing about the May Day Tournament.

I looked out the window of the truck while Michael talked, sometimes paying more attention to the passing landscape of trees and farms and the mile after mile of tree stumps and saplings sprouting to take their place. Michael paused only when Deiter would interrupt with a question, and then resumed his story.

During the trip to England, Michael said he received his standard army pay of eleven dollars and seventy cents per month, a stipend for food of ninety cents a day, and bonuses for winning.

Deiter asked Michael how many tournaments he won. Michael said he was pretty sure he won six of the nine tournaments he played in, and added that he rarely spent any money except the meal allocation. Most of the other Russian team members spent their pay visiting pubs and brothels. Michael said he would tag along periodically, but as a Pole, his comrades treated him as a second-class outcast they were forced to tolerate. Michael said he was clearly not one of them, and never got comfortable around the pompous, arrogant, and officious Russian officers who made up a large part of the group. He said he preferred to walk the city and visit museums, often accompanied by his new friend Witold.

Michael said he liked Witold immediately, and could easily make him laugh with subtle derogatory comments about his "brother Russians." Michael described Witold as short, disheveled, bespectacled, and five years older. It occurred to me that Witold would have been a sharp contrast to Michael who was tall, slim, and probably impeccably attired in his dress Czarist uniform, which he said he was required to wear as a Russian Army ambassador. Witold traveled with the Russian and British teams aboard the same train and continued to do so throughout the tour. Michael said talking with Witold broke the tedium. I empathized, after just traveling with Deiter from New York.

I was particularly interested in Michael's description of the series of events that led up to the First World War. Although I was four years old at the start of the war, I remember my father talking about the same things. I listened and looked out at the occasional passing farm and cluster of buildings pretending to be a town. I bounced every time the truck passed over the top of the culverts and bridges built across what seemed to be thousands of creeks, rivers, and rills that flowed under the roads of northern Wisconsin.

Michael said that he heard the first talk of war while in England on June 29, 1914. That was when news of the assassination of the Austria-Hungary Archduke Francis Ferdinand and his wife reached London. Although this unnerving event led people to speculate about war, Michael said even his commanding officer didn't seriously think it would lead to hostilities. He said Witold had even joked about it, saying, "The Archduke was shot, big deal. Austria is a big country. I'll bet they can find a replacement."

Michael said evidently the senior Russian military staff had a different view and shortly after the assassination, his unit received orders to return to Russia. The army was being mobilized. But a day or two later the orders were rescinded and their tournaments continued. The following week rumors spread that they would likely be ordered back to Russia again. It was at that point that Michael said it became apparent to him that war was imminent. He began to worry about getting home and about his family. Michael said his Russian teammates were eager for war, adding, "If they only knew what they were hoping for."

I remember that ride from the station, and hell, that whole year that I was a Chickadee, as if it happened yesterday, probably because so much happened during that short period. But on that drive I began to learn of Michael's ability to remember everything—dates, names, places, and specific events, even the most mundane. The more I got to know him, the more I appreciated his intellect. He is the smartest person I've ever been around.

Michael said it was August 1st, 1914, at a train station near London, when he received news that Germany had declared war on Russia. This time there would be no reprieve. The tour was cancelled and Michael said he was informed by the commanding officer that they would receive orders soon regarding deployment.

Shortly after that he heard that the British had sunk a German mine-laying ship. Michael said he knew if Germany invaded Russian territory that their home would likely be near the front, and that any invasion of Russia from the west had to go through Poland.

Deiter interrupted Michael. "Just a couple of weeks after that Jan left home to fight the Germans. It was Russia that killed him though."

Michael shook his head and asked, "How long before Mother and Father were killed?"

"About a year and a half," Deiter said.

Michael paused a moment, then continued to tell us about Witold. Michael said during his final weeks in England, Witold became a very good friend and the only person he could really trust. Michael and his Russian chess team returned to London to wait for a ship to take them back to Russia. While Michael was organizing his bag in his barrack preparing to disembark, Witold came up behind him.

"Desert," Witold whispered to Michael. "Stay in England. I'll see after you. You're going back to serve as fodder for the Russian army. Us Poles are the first ones thrown at the enemy. Only when they're out of Poles will the Russians fight. What good can you be to your family dead? Here we can work together to get them the hell out of that mess."

Michael said he told Witold that he couldn't stay. But Witold was undeterred and answered, "Of course you can. I did."

Michael said he was concerned the British wouldn't accept a deserter from an ally. But Witold said not to worry because he could arrange it. There was a large Polish contingency in England and they were eager to get political asylum for Poles.

"I was in the army Deiter, I couldn't desert," Michael said. "They would have retaliated against you and the family. Witold told me to just think about it and gave me a note with his address if I had to reach him."

Michael described London as chaotic. The military was on full alert, troops were being transported, enlistees lined up for blocks at recruitment centers, and all forms of transportation were subject to immediate and indefinite command of the military.

Michael said the only reason he wasn't shipped back to Russia then was that despite their orders, the Russians couldn't arrange for transportation. He described several false starts, with officers ordering the men to prepare to leave only to receive orders to stand down until further notice. He thought it was on August 7 that the Russian chess team received a dispatch from the British Council, which said something like *German Army has invaded Russia. Pushing east. Western Russian Army overrun.* At that point Michael said he realized there was no way he would be able to get home. No able-bodied soldier would be going anywhere but to the front.

"We finally got word in the middle of August that a Russian cruiser was making its way from the Mediterranean toward London to collect the Russian soldiers in England," Michael said.

The following morning he was ordered to report to his commanding officer. Changing his voice to that of a gruff, officious Russian, Michael mimicked the officer, "Small matter to clear up. Your enlistment was for six months, expired August sixth. However, not to worry. You will remain a proud Russian soldier and will be conscripted for the duration of hostilities upon arrival of the paperwork from Moscow in a couple of days. That is all." Deiter laughed at Michael's exaggerated caricature.

Michael said he hadn't entirely absorbed the importance of that meeting until later, when he realized that his papers indicated he was no longer in the service of the Great Russian Army.

"You can't desert an army that has officially informed you your enlistment period has expired. I knew the intent was to extend my term of service but at that moment I was out of the army and without orders. With the news of the German invasion of Russia through Poland making steady progress east, I knew they would be at our home soon, if they hadn't reached it already."

A window of opportunity had opened for Michael and he

realized the reasons he gave Witold for not staying in England were no longer valid. At that moment Michael was a *former* Russian soldier and Polish citizen whose home was occupied, or about to be, by an invading foreign force. He was an ideal candidate for asylum.

Michael said, "I couldn't be considered a deserter. Well at least not until the Russians tracked me down and personally delivered my papers and sealed my fate. I often took walks, so wasn't missed when I left the compound early the next morning. I went to Witold's apartment. It was seven in the morning and he was just getting up. I told him of the new developments, emphasizing that until my new orders arrived, I was not officially a Russian soldier."

Michael told Witold that he decided he could do more for his family by staying alive, earning money, and preparing to step in to help as soon as the opportunity occurred. Going back to Russia as a Pole, only to be thrown onto the front lines without any military training, was in his view stupid and probably suicidal. He also agreed with Witold's view that German occupation of Poland was probably preferable to Russian rule. Michael summarized Witold's assessment, "The Germans were shitty, but the Russians shittier, so fighting against German occupation would be counterproductive."

Michael said he thought that if he stayed in England and the Russians found him, there is no doubt they would've carted him back to Russia, to either face a firing squad or be assigned to one of the assault brigades destined to charge the German lines with few arms and little ammunition. Michael said it was Witold who offered a solution—go to America.

Michael said Witold was convincing. He reminded Michael that the Yanks were neutral, and their ships came and went every day from London and Dublin. The Russians could scour Britain all they want, but the Russians had a war to fight and might not put that much effort in trying to find a wayward chess player.

The more he thought about it, the more Michael said he believed that Witold was right. While America was too far away for him to help the family immediately, at least he would be out of the reach of the Russians and it would be a safe place to work for good pay. He would need the money to help his family. Michael emphasized to Deiter that it was a tough decision because he felt he was running away when his family needed help the most.

Deiter assured Michael that he did the right thing. "You'd have been no good to anyone dead and that's what you'd be. There isn't anything you could have done to help Mother and Father, or Jan for that matter. Those things were going to happen no matter what. And me, I don't know what I would've done if you weren't already here with a job for me. Probably would still be working the Szeryng's farm."

"Yeah, but I didn't know it then. I feel guilty about just looking out for myself," Michael said.

Michael said he had earned enough money to execute his plan with the equivalent of two hundred and eighty dollars left from his army pay, meal money, and bonuses. Because mail was normally slow and unreliable, with the war starting it would be even worse. He decided to leave communication with the family up to Witold's network. Witold had connections with Polish nationals who traveled between England and Poland. Michael hoped they could get a letter through, but was concerned that the letter might be intercepted by the Russians. Michael said Witold's solution was to only say where he was going and leave all names out of the letter. The missing information would make the letter meaningless to the Russians, but Michael's family would understand.

"We got that letter. The second one came a month later and told us you were going to work here. That's the only way I would have been able to find you. Say, how much farther is the camp anyway?" Deiter asked.

"We're about halfway. The roads are really rutted up ahead so we won't make very good time."

Won't make very good time. *(Image 008 from the collection of the German Settlement History Inc., Ogema, WI)*

Michael had been talking for nearly half an hour. With the exception of a man and a boy on a horse-drawn wagon, I don't remember seeing another person along the road or on any of the farms we passed. My first impression of this area was that it seemed desolate, like the German landscape after the war.

Deiter asked Michael if he came over on a freighter like he did.

"Nope. I bought a third-class ticket on a Cunard Steamship sailing out of Liverpool, England. I left August 17, 1914, for New York. The ticket cost two hundred and ten dollars. I was worried right up to boarding the ship that the British might refuse to let me go. I was worried for nothing. They just stamped my papers and off I went. Once on board I got a message from Witold.

Bon Voyage. Two Russians stopped by my flat this morning right after you left. They inquired as to your whereabouts. I told them I last saw you with a bottle of vodka and a woman in Soho. They instructed me to let you know that you were to report to your commanding officer immediately and were confined to barracks until the transport arrived to take you back to Russia. Stan Lisek will meet you when you arrive in New York. He has a job arranged for you doing lumber surveys and estimates for a logging operation in Wisconsin. I will wire you when I know more. Best of luck! Witold.

When he arrived in New York, he met Lisek and learned about his job with the Thunder Logging Company. Michael told us his job would be to assess the amount and value of standing and cut timber. They were logging near Watersmeet, Michigan, at the time. The owner, Sam Slaby, was a friend of Lisek who Witold knew from Krakow. Lisek introduced Michael to Slaby, who needed a timber assessor, "so I guess I was his man."

Over time Michael said he learned that it was taking Slaby's foreman weeks to walk the land, inventory the tree species and sizes, and estimate the board feet for property that Slaby owned timber rights to. Despite taking all that time, Slaby still couldn't trust the accuracy of the assessments. One of the first things Slaby told Michael was to try to get him numbers as fast as he could, but be accurate, especially when looking at land he wanted to buy. Everybody wanted the best tracts of second-growth lumber, so when they were available it was critical to act fast.

Michael said he could tell Slaby was skeptical of his first few reports since he gave his estimates so quickly. But Michael said he was confident in his work because assessing forests and doing some calculations was exactly what he was studying in forestry at the technical college. With all those years of playing chess he got pretty good at doing calculations in his head. It seemed to pay off. Michael developed a kind of assessment shorthand. He described how he would first walk the land, periodically stop in a part of the forest that was most representative of the tract, and pace off twenty-two yards. By visualizing that line as one side of a square, he would be looking at one-tenth of an acre. By counting the trees in that area and multiplying by ten, violà, he had the average number of trees per acre. Then it was just a matter of sizing up the girth and height of the typical tree in his square and multiplying the number of twelve-inch boards that could be sawed from each ten-foot log.

"Will, I think my brother here is just showing off, don't you?" Deiter said.

"You did ask what I do here, and that's what I do," Michael answered.

Deiter said he preferred to just be swinging an axe and asked Michael what kinds of trees were lumbered here. Michael told him it was a lot of mixed hardwood, mostly maple, and that virtually all first-growth pine had been clear-cut years ago. The river bottoms and lowlands surrounding lakes have tamarack, hemlock, and cedar. Areas that had burned over have good growths of jack pine. They do well after forest fires. He said that once in a while they would get a stand of pine, but that Deiter better keep his axe sharp because he'd be chopping down a lot of maple and birch.

Deiter complained saying he hated cutting hardwoods. He had to cut a lot of oak when he was on the rail and bridge repair crew. "Chop for an hour and hardly make a dent in those damn trees," he said.

Seeming to try to improve Deiter's enthusiasm for the job, Michael told Deiter that Slaby had sent him out to investigate an area rumored to be extremely well wooded. Michael didn't think Slaby would ever get a chance to buy it, but that it was a virgin stand of white pine near the Chippewa River. Somehow that stand was overlooked during the cutover. The 820-acre tract included 480 acres of virgin white pine. Michael said it was mostly high ground surrounded on three sides by a chain of lakes. It was owned by the Wisconsin Northern Railroad, and the railroad was keeping it in case they needed to build a spur off the main line running east-west to link up with a new copper field. Slaby told Michael that he would try his damnedest to buy it, but that it was important to keep his survey quiet.

Michael said he tried to find out more but the railroad land agent wouldn't discuss the parcel. The railroad owned tens of thousands of acres in the area. They were granted ownership of all land one mile on both sides of any new track they laid. With that much land, mostly acquired fifty to sixty years before, the records were unreliable at best. When inquiries came, if the railroad's land agent knew where the paperwork was, he could sell the parcel if the price was right and if the railroad didn't have plans for it. He had incentive to sell land approved by the railroad because they'd pay him a commission on every sale, and he could get a periodic bribe for doing a buyer a favor.

Michael said he didn't work for Slaby anymore, that he was killed six months before. Lumbering was a lot more civil now than it was back in 1870s and '80s, but there was still a good share of ruthlessness and greed.

From what I could understand from Michael's story, Slaby had been checking the status of logging at a worksite. The crew was taking out a nice stand of red maple and making good progress. Michael was away "walking some swamp near the St. Croix." Slaby decided to check out the next two sections to figure how many months it would take his crew to finish logging it. He must have noticed that the survey stakes at the northeast corner of his property were moved a quarter of mile back into his land. Another crew had set up operations and was clear-cutting Slaby's section.

No one's sure what happened next but Michael assumed that the old man approached the other crew. Michael said Slaby could be ornery and was sure he'd be riled up over the survey lines. They probably shouted at each other. Maybe made some threats. Slaby would have headed back into the woods to get to camp, probably thinking about how he would bring his crew up there to teach those bastards a thing or two, and then sue their asses. Michael laughed at his own account, adding that if nothing else Slaby was predictable. He said that Slaby reminded him a little of his father, hard-working, honest, "a lot of bark, little bite."

Michael became more serious when he told us that at some point after Slaby turned to leave he was shot in the back and killed. It took three weeks before they found his body. It was under a ten-foot high pile of branches that had been stripped from his own timber. A full 120 acres of Slaby's land had been cleared by the timber thieves. His body was found when it began to decompose during a warm spell. "The smell guided us right to him." The sheriff investigated, but there wasn't much evidence and no witnesses. No one was ever charged.

Reflecting, Michael told Deiter, "You know that could have been me. It should have been. But Slaby just couldn't wait 'til I got back from looking over those sections west of here. I don't know what I would have done if I saw a crew stealing timber."

"Does that happen a lot?" Deiter asked.

"Stealing timber, yes, killing no," Michael said. "The survey stakes are just too easy to move and out here in the middle of nowhere the chances of being caught are slim. By the time you get the land re-surveyed they're long gone. It's hard to prosecute. Most of the time you just lose twenty to forty acres of timber or somebody gets beaten to a pulp. But that's it."

After Slaby was killed, the Thunder Logging Company was sold at auction, at what Michael thought was a fraction of its real value. Jack Seely, owner of Seely Lumber and Land Company, bought the business. With the purchase came all the land and timber rights that Slaby owned. Timber already cut by Slaby's company would be purchased for market value after it was inventoried at the mill.

After buying Slaby's business, Jack Seely and his son,

Jason, hired on Tom Nelson, Slaby's foreman, Michael, and about a third of the Thunder Logging crew. Michael said that Seely still owed Slaby's old crew some back pay and payment for all the lumber cut at Thunder Logging but that hadn't been inventoried at the sawmill yet.

Jason was Michael's age when he took over the management of the Seely Company from his father. Michael said it was pretty clear to him that Jack didn't think Jason was ready. He had overheard Jack telling his foreman that Jason "was too easily distracted, too interested in women, too lazy, and had way too high an opinion *of his own* opinion."

Shortly after that, Jack Seely had a stroke that paralyzed most of his right side. Michael said it was sad to watch the old man struggle to get around and try to communicate with his speech slurred and slow. At that point, he had to put Jason in charge.

Michael said he respected Jack Seely. Everyone who knew him said the old man was a real hard driver—worked eighteen-hour days and often stayed in his office all night. He speculated that the pace of work, all those cigars he smoked, and his girth finally caught up with him. He had a temper, too. The last time Michael saw Jack, he said the old man was all riled up. Spitting and slurring, shouting at the foreman, "Damn it. Why duth thith country alwath need a damn war for anybody to make any money?" Michael quoting the best he could while mimicking the old man's speech.

Deiter asked Michael what Jason was like. Michael said one of the reasons Jack was so angry that day was because his investments in stocks were going down. Jason had been trying to get the old man to buy cut-over land cheap and sell it for a profit to immigrants, and get out of the logging business altogether. The drop in the value of Jack's stocks was one of the reasons Jason was trying to expand the Seely Land Division. Jason's friend, Joseph Habrich, was an agent with the Sanborn Land Company near Eagle River.

"Joe comes here often bragging to Jason that he has sold nearly one hundred separate forty-acre plots near Velebit to Croatians," Michael said. "He would swagger in laughing and tell Jason, '*It ain't my fault if the pictures they saw made 'em think that they was buyin' cleared land ready for planting.*'"

Michael said another friend of Jason, Ben Faast, was doing the same thing at the Wisconsin Colonization Company in Ojibwa. Once Croats and others arrived at the actual landsite and saw that it was just stumps and rocks, it was too late to turn around, and they had little recourse. No one's going to give them a refund. Most stay and try to make a living out of their acres while the land companies make small fortunes.

The only characteristic Jack and his son Jason shared was their height. Both were about six feet tall. But, Jack had a presence, a real intensity. Men listened to Jack. His orders were obeyed. He was frumpy, didn't give much thought to his appearance, and frankly could give a shit how he looked or what people thought of him. Jason on the other hand was arrogant, pompous, self-absorbed, and preening. Michael said you could tell by the way Jack talked to Jason that there was a combination of contempt and disappointment.

Jason got a business degree after going to school in Minnesota, even though it took him four-and-a-half years to finish the three-year business program. Michael said it was clear that Jason didn't seem to like him very much.

Deiter asked Michael what he thought of Jason, and what the camp was like. Michael said he was still trying to size Jason up, and the camp was a combination of two crews consisting of locals and immigrant workers. Lots of Finns and Swedes, but there was someone from virtually every European country. He thought Deiter would fit right in.

With that Michael announced, "You can see for yourself. We're just about there."

11

We emerged from the thick forest on both sides of the snow-covered, rutted road and entered a clearing. I got the first glimpse of my new home. There were several buildings, the most prominent a barn and what looked like a bunkhouse. Between the buildings was an open area, with the snow packed down and deep ruts frozen in time from when heavy vehicles drove through what was then mud. The woods ended abruptly along a line running from the camp to the top of a distant hill. There, only stumps and branches poking up through the snow remained of the forest. The gray sky, dirty snow, and unpainted buildings made the place look ominous and bleak. It was late afternoon and some of the crews were heading out of the forest. Others were in the process of wrapping up their day's work, creating a din of chopping, sawing, horses whinnying, snow crunching, and men cussing and shouting. I felt completely out of place, and despite being surrounded by people, alone. I tried to stay as close to Deiter as I could, without looking like I was trying to.

The first to approach the truck was one of the lumbermen. He introduced himself to Deiter as Oscar Nykanenju. He had brown, almost black hair, but his thick moustache and beard stubble were a mix of red and yellow. His barrel chest strained against the buttons on his green wool shirt. His canvas coat was flung over his shoulder, and shirt sleeves rolled up revealed a large bandage on his right arm.

Despite the bandage, based on the look on Deiter's face, the man evidently nearly crushed Deiter's hand when he shook it.

"Hi, I'm Nyka," he said to Deiter, then turned to me.

He vigorously rubbed my hair with his massive hand, poked me in the chest, and joked that he had axes bigger than me.

"You gonna be the new Chickadee? The last one either ran away or got lost in the woods. Ain't been seen for a month. With the snow here already, we'll need the sled lanes clear all the way to the railroad line," Nyka said.

I told him I would take the Chickadee job if that was the only job available for a boy.

Nyka laughed, "We've already got too many boys here tryin' to be loggers. We need more Finns." He called over to the foreman, "Hey Bundy, looks like we got 'arselves a new Chickadee."

"Yup. Mike just told me."

"I'll show 'em what a Chickadee does," Nyka said. Bundy nodded.

I was curious about the last Chickadee and wanted to ask why he just up and left. What became of him? Didn't anyone care where he was? But I chose to keep my questions to myself for the time being.

I sensed Michael's coolness toward Nyka, despite the Finn's friendliness. Michael rejoined us and repeated that Bundy agreed that they needed a new Chickadee and as long as I behaved myself and did my work, I'd be welcome. I could bunk in the kitchen or barn, whichever I preferred.

Michael and Deiter said goodbye to Nyka, and the brothers walked with me in tow over to the mess hall. They found the camp's cook. She had been kneading dough for bread and biscuits, humming while she worked in the light of a single kerosene lantern. A white cloud of airborne flour dust engulfed her in a foggy glow. She was a very short and very round black woman, wearing a torn apron and a light pink dress.

Michael made the introductions. The kitchen belonged to the cook, Matilda McPhearson, who everyone knew as Mattie or Cookee. Mattie had cooked at a couple of different logging camps before Seely. She was smiling and after wiping her hands on her apron, shook our hands using both of hers and warmly welcomed Deiter and me to her kitchen. Taking me by the arm Mattie led me, Michael, and Deiter to a small storage room behind the stove. On the way she told me some of the kitchen rules, the most important being that no one could get any food at any time other than breakfast and dinner. Mattie said that with their voracious appetites, the men would keep her hopping twenty-four hours a day.

We entered a tiny room. At the end of a narrow cot against the outside wall was a small heap of clothes, a pair of boots, an open cigar box of lead toy soldiers and odds and ends.

"This here's where Chickadees stay," Mattie said. "The stuff over yonder belonged to the las' Chickadee. S'pose you kin have it since he ain't come back."

The room was too small for the four of us to crowd in. Michael and Mattie stood in the doorway while Deiter and I wandered in. Deiter knocked his head on one of the twenty bunches of onions hanging from an exposed crossbeam. He ducked under the next bunch and leaned against a wooden box the size of one of the big tree stumps I saw scattered across the landscape when we drove from the train station.

"Taters," Mattie said, gesturing toward the box.

Mattie told us that the last boy, Chester, just up and left. No one knew where he'd run off to. Good kid. Max Adler brought him in last spring. Was the kid of one of the whores in town. Evidently she didn't know what to do with the kid and thought the camp would be a better place for him to stay.

Then Mattie looked at me and said, "O'well, looks like we got r'selves a bran' spankin' new un. Room ain't much, but bein' behind the stove and me cookin' all the time, why it's right comfturble. Better 'n bein' in the barn with Abraham, though he likes bein' there wit' the critters."

Nyka reappeared behind Michael and Mattie and barged in, interrupting Mattie.

"Come on, kid," he said. "I'll edjekate ya on the fine art of Chickadeean. You can unpack later. Kid's gotta know what the hell he's doin'."

Nyka ignored the contemptuous looks he got from Michael and Mattie and led me out the door. I followed him outside toward the woods where men had been working when we arrived. We stopped at a small shed next to a hand pump over the horse trough. He stopped only long enough to scoop up a bucket with a ladle inside. He turned to the pump, hung the bucket by a ridge on the tap, and pushed the handle of the pump up and down twice. Water gushed into the bucket.

"Don't matter how cold it gets. This here pump won't freeze up. If you try pumpin' it and nothin' comes out, you gotta prime it. Jus' pour a little water down the top of the pump right here," Nyka said.

He gestured toward the deep ruts in the snow leading to the logging trails. Nyka explained that although the company had tractors, they were impossible to start when the temperatures plummeted and they got stuck repeatedly when the snow piled up. The steep hills, moraines, and littering of rocks made horse-drawn sleds the more reliable way of moving hardwood logs to the rails and pine logs to the river.

Nyka and I walked together down the center of the trail as he explained my new duties. While he talked I watched him reach in his pocket and pull out a small blunt screwdriver. I tried to stay next to him as we walked on the trail.

"Them horses eat a lot'a hay, boy. You know what happens then?"

Not knowing where Nyka was going with the question, I shrugged.

"Well they takes a dump tha's what. Horse apples is everywhere on the trail. When they freeze solid, they're like hittin' a rock. It jars the sled. When that happens, them

69

logs piled twenty feet high move, sometimes bustin' the chains holdin' 'em or shiftin' enough to tip over the whole damn thing."

Without warning, my feet shot out from under me and I fell hard on the ice-packed trail.

"That's why I walk here in the middle, boy. The whole idea is that them rails on the sled can slide real nice, just like you did."

The leather soles on my boots were like skates on the snowpack and ice. I fell three or four more times during our tour. Walking with one foot in the deeper snow in the middle and the other foot on the side of the trail didn't help much.

"It's gonna take ya all day to ice the trails if you're on your ass half the time," Nyka teased. "Look over here," he pointed, "nice collection of horse apples. Now you take this here screwdriver and use it to chip it loose, like this." Using his hand as a hammer on the back of the screwdriver he neatly chipped one of the "apples," which flew up clear off the trail.

Gotta keep the tracks clear. *(Image BK067 from the collection of the German Settlement History Inc., Ogema, WI)*

"Then you jes' take a ladle of water and pour it on. The cold does the rest. The las' Chickadee liked to use a knife, but you use this here screwdriver and it'll do a good job for ya."

Sure enough, within seconds, an icy sheen covered the small amount of "apple" residue left frozen fast to the track.

"Here, now you try." Nyka handed me the bucket and screwdriver.

I followed his example exactly, but when I used my hand to hammer the screwdriver, it just flecked off a tiny chip. I had to repeat the process five or six times before I finally dislodged it.

"Use them muscles, boy."

Eventually I cleared a majority of the heap, then splashed water on it. The palm of my hand was starting to throb from repeatedly striking the handle of the screwdriver.

"Yer using too much water. You'll use up the whole bucket before yer half done. But as long as there's snow you can always add it to the water. But don't put in too much or it'll just soak up what water ya still has. Can't use slush. That freezes too uneven. Takes a lotta snow to make a bucket a' water. Once it gets winter cold that water is gonna freeze up while yer out here. Use the screwdriver to chip through the ice that forms in yer bucket. You get started before sunup and before the crew gets out here, so you gotta eat yer breakfast real early."

While we walked to the next spot to clear, Nyka talked about the merging of the Thunder and Seely logging camps. Although I just heard Michael tell Deiter about the camp, I just listened as Nyka gave his take. Nyka was a Seely man. Jack Seely moved his foreman and some of his men to join the Thunder crew at their main camp because the timber was better than on the parcel they were logging, and it was a good way for Seely to keep an eye on the Thunder crew. Nyka said he liked most of the Thunder crew but thought Michael was a little "uppity."

While walking the trail Nyka asked me where I was from, where my parents were, how did I end up at the Seely camp

71

and the like. But being timid, shy, and scared as hell, I answered as briefly as possible, asked no questions of my own and volunteered little.

When we arrived back at camp, the men were filing toward the mess hall. Dinner was being served. I realized how hungry I was as soon as I smelled dinner and got right behind Nyka as we reached the mess hall door. Nyka stopped abruptly and waved his arm toward the kitchen.

"Chickadees don't eat with the loggers, boy. You eat with Cookee an' her kid."

I had to wait in the back of the kitchen while Mattie served dinner to the men. When they were finished, she told me to help Abraham with the dishes. When we put away the last of the pots, Mattie placed three plates on the small table in the kitchen. I didn't know what we were going to eat—the loggers didn't leave anything. All the bowls and platters Mattie brought back from the mess hall were empty. She reached into the warming compartment of the huge wood stove and pulled out a sausage and a pile of boiled potatoes for us. Abraham and I ate while Mattie chatted away, stopping just long enough to ask a question, take a bite of her supper, and then embark on another story remotely related to something we said. I think she was doing her best to make me feel more comfortable. She had a mother's sense of my apprehension.

She laughed at all her stories. Abraham smiled and nodded knowingly, as though he had heard them many times before. I just tried to take it all in while quickly devouring the best meal I had in weeks.

Just before sending Abraham and me off to bed, Mattie turned more serious and said, "That Nyka is one son-of-a-gun when he gits mad. You best watch out. Never seen a man go from bein' all nice and all, to puttin' a knife to your belly 'cause ya crossed 'em. Mean drunk, too. I reck'un you'll be fine so long as yer careful."

He had been nice to me, so I just passed it off.

12

At four-thirty the next morning Mattie shook me awake. I was cocooned tightly in a wool blanket and dirty quilt. "You better get somethin' in ya before ya go out," Mattie said. I had not slept well. Nightmares woke me up repeatedly during the night, and I just couldn't seem to get warm. I got up in the middle of the night to put on another pair of socks and laid my coat over the blankets, all to no avail. When I woke up to Mattie's voice in the darkness, I was completely disoriented and panicky. I couldn't remember where I was. Once she knew I was awake she hurried back to the kitchen to continue preparing for breakfast.

I sat at the end of the bed in my long johns and socks for a moment, trying to gather my thoughts about what I was supposed to do next.

I heard Mattie call from the kitchen, "Git yerself some pants on and git a move on or ya won't have time to eat nuthin."

While dressing in the dark I stepped on a lead soldier that had dropped on the floor. I had played with them just before I fell asleep the night before. Mattie must have heard me stumble.

Laughing she called out to me, "Now don't ya be hurtin' any a'my taters or onions in there."

Mattie had made me a bowl of boiled oats from the hundred pound bag that was stored in the barn for the horses. They were awful and I must have made a face when I took the first bite. Mattie saw it and, smiling, she reached for a jar high on a shelf next to the stove, undid the cap, and dripped a little maple syrup over the oats. She said I was just like Abraham.

While I ate, Mattie said she heard me talking in my sleep and tossing and turning all night. I knew I was restless. I was trying to remember Nyka's instructions and the orientation of the camp and had trouble falling asleep, slept fitfully when I finally nodded off, and had a recurring nightmare about my mother.

Mattie assured me, "After walkin' them trails all mornin' and breathin' that cold air, you'll sleep like a baby."

Abraham opened the back door to the kitchen after walking the short distance from the barn. He sat down without a word. A bowl of boiled oats materialized as if out of thin air in front of him, complete with an amber trickle of syrup.

I remember slipping into German only a couple of times. That first morning I said "*Guten morgen*" to Abraham before correcting myself. While on the ship coming to America, many of the passengers passed the time by trying to learn as much English as they could. My mother was no exception and made sure we both learned some English before we left Germany and practiced while we were en route. Having learned English before we left was particularly important when Mother was sick with the influenza and in the aftermath. I needed to understand what was happening, and the army medic on board and the ship's crew spoke English. After Mother died and I snapped out of depression, I tried to learn quickly and got extra time to practice during the quarantine period on the boat and in New York. Deiter spoke German, as well as Polish and Russian, and he picked up English very easily. He was the perfect tutor and the two of us practiced speaking English to each other during the ten-day train trip from New York to Hayward. Deiter told me he wanted to become fluent enough to converse. He feared he would be less employable without the skill and wanted to appear less like a recent immigrant. I guess I did, too.

Abraham and I didn't speak much during breakfast until Abraham mentioned something about the horses. I really perked up and started firing questions at Abraham. "Which horse is your favorite?" "What are their names?" "Can you ride them?" Before Abraham could answer any of them, Mattie returned and ordered both of us out of the kitchen and directed us to get to work. As Abraham slowly headed to the barn, I shouted after him, "Can I help you later?"

Abraham shrugged and said over his shoulder that I could if I wanted to. That was all I needed to hear to have my spirits raised for the first time in weeks. I grabbed my bucket, ladle, and screwdriver, filled the bucket at the pump and walked toward the trail.

It was five-fifteen and still dark, except for a faint light from a sliver of a moon reflecting off the snow cover. It took several seconds for my eyes to adjust. Even then it was difficult to see well enough to make my way down the trail. I paused at the top of the trail. Terror set in. I was about to walk into a strange forest in the dark, by myself. I could hear the faint sounds of movement deep in the forest. *I can't do this.* This is the same forest the last Chickadee disappeared into, never to be heard from again.

It was only when one of the loggers unceremoniously banged open the bunkhouse door to take a leak that I snapped out of it. It was bad enough being a Chickadee, but worse to be a chicken. Turns out I had a greater fear of Nyka, Deiter, and the other men thinking I was too frightened to even do a Chickadee's job than I did of going into the woods alone. Reluctantly the new Chickadee embarked down the trail into the darkness.

I hadn't gotten twenty yards before I slipped and fell head first down a small incline, splashing water as I tumbled, soaking my pants. I was frightened, wet and cold, and hadn't even started yet. Since I was still close to the pump I headed back and refilled the bucket. I tried to proceed with more caution this time using the center of the trail and walking in the snow rather than taking the slick ruts for the sled's runners.

75

To take my mind off what might be lurking just out of sight in the woods, I thought about getting back and going to the barn with Abraham and the horses. It took nearly two hours for me to finally finish my first circuit around the one-and-a-half miles of serpentine trails. I was exhausted, freezing, and soaking wet.

I returned the bucket to the back door of the kitchen and ran toward the barn. The sun was just coming up. The sky was light but the woods gave up darkness reluctantly. The men finished breakfast and were filing out of the mess hall heading to the bunkhouse for their tools and coats. When I got to the barn, I was disappointed to see Abraham emerge leading a team of horses hitched to the huge sled used to haul the logs. I ran over to help, but ended up just watching. Max, the company teamster, jumped onto the board that served as a seat and encouraged the huge draft animals toward the forest.

The boys workin' in the barn. *(Image 777 from the collection of the German Settlement History Inc., Ogema, WI)*

I returned to the barn with Abraham, intent on learning more about the horses and hoping to make myself welcome. Abraham did not require ingratiating. He was happy to have help and company. Unfortunately I couldn't stay long. Once I stopped moving around, the cold air and wet clothes chilled me to the bone. It took me half an hour standing in front of the stove in the kitchen to warm up.

13

A couple of days after arriving in camp, Deiter came to my room to see how things were going. I was sitting on my bed barefoot. All three pair of socks I owned were still wet from my route and hanging near the stove. Deiter saw them when he passed the stove on his way to my room.

"I think you need to waterproof those boots of yours," he said, and told me to come over to the bunkhouse where he'd help me put some mink oil on them.

I took him up on his offer later that morning. When I entered the bunkhouse, a couple of the men said, "Hey, this ain't no place for a Chickadee."

Deiter told them he invited me and why I was there. I guess as long as a Chickadee had an invitation from a logger it was okay to be there, because nothing more was said. Deiter sat me in a corner near his bunk and gave me a small covered tin of mink oil and a rag. I worked slowly, rubbing oil first onto my boots, then Michael's and Deiter's.

A man I hadn't seen before came into the bunkhouse. He greeted a few of the men, who said, "Hi Jason." He walked over to Michael.

"You did the assessing for Thunder right?' he asked Michael. "We need to know how much timber you boys cut that's on the ground so I can finish the deal on that two-bit operation of yours. How many board feet of lumber you figure you have here?"

"I haven't completed the inventory, but I can give you an estimate if you'd like," Michael answered.

"Don't bother, I can tell you how much is here just by looking over this half-assed operation. There are five hundred thousand board feet here, tops."

Michael told him that although he hadn't finished the inventory, he was pretty sure there was close to eight hundred and fifty thousand board feet.

That seemed to make Jason mad. "You're crazy, or don't have any idea what the hell you're doing," Jason said.

"Would you like to bet on that?" Michael asked.

"Bet with what? You got a piss pot you want to wager?"

A couple of men from his crew laughed, but no one from the Thunder Logging crew did.

"Well, I'd prefer to bet a hundred dollars that there are at least eight hundred thousand board feet of lumber on the ground, on the sleds, and at the river with the Thunder Logging mark. We can use the final accounting from the mill as the official tally."

Bunkhouse. *(Image BK0001 from the collection of the German Settlement History Inc., Ogema, WI)*

"Is this Polack good for a hundred bucks?" Jason asked, looking at the Thunder Logging crew. There were supportive nods. "You're on, Polack."

When Jason left, one of the men told Michael that no one ever calls Jason's bluff and Michael sure as hell pissed him off.

Tom Nelson, the foreman of the old Thunder crew, knew Jason well and told Michael that Jason usually just plows over anyone who disagrees by using threats, insults, bluster, and bullshit. Then Tom warned, "That asshole won't forget this, Michael."

Tom told Michael that he thought Jason was trying to cheat Slaby's widow and all of the Thunder crew out of thousands of dollars in back pay. All Jason had to do was undervalue the timber that was part of the purchase of Thunder. According to the purchase terms, Jason had to pay for the timber already cut and the wages due to the Thunder crew for cutting it.

If the actual amount of cut lumber turned out more than the low estimate Jason used at the time of the purchase, the contract called for him to pay the difference between his estimate and the actual amount of timber.

Michael knew his estimate was pretty close. Tom warned Michael that Jason would do what he could to be sure the assessed board feet of the inventory was as low as possible.

Tom asked Michael how much money they were talking about. Michael said that Jason would make twenty-two dollars per thousand board feet and that he was underestimating by three hundred thousand feet, or about sixty-six hundred dollars. He only paid eleven thousand for the whole company, and if you add in the inventory and back pay due, he would owe another nine thousand. Jason would try to pay as little of that as he could get away with.

14

A couple of weeks later while making my morning circuit, I saw men from Jason's crew working in the piles of maple logs previously cut by the Thunder crew. No one was ever out on the trails before breakfast, and I thought it was odd. After they left, I circled back and nosed around to see what they were doing. The best I could tell was that they were using their axes to chip off the Thunder crew markings and reapplying the Seely mark. I remembered the day Jason came to the bunkhouse, the bet, and what Tom had said. I figured what I saw was important.

I found Michael just before he climbed into the company truck and told him about it.

"I knew Jason would try to pull something," Michael said. He thanked me for coming to him and told me that what I saw was Jason trying to steal the Thunder timber inventory. He must have thought it was important for me to understand because he took the time to explain how the inventory worked.

He said that logs from dozens of operations like ours went to the big mills at the same time. The only way for the mill to be sure they paid the right company for the right logs was to have each log marked by the loggers who cut it. Each team of loggers had an axe with a flat end engraved with a team number. Before sending the logs to the mill, the company would add their mark, usually initials, to each log cut by their teams. He said this worked just like branding cattle.

By tallying the number of the logs, size, and type, the mill established an accurate record of how much to pay each company for their timber.

I asked him what he was going to do. Michael said he wasn't sure. But that he would tell Tom, because Tom had a lot to lose from Jason changing the marks. Tom had a small stake in the Thunder Logging Company. Michael said Slaby told him that he gave Tom fifteen percent equity in the company

Switchin' the marks. *(Image BK035 from the collection of the German Settlement History Inc., Ogema, WI)*

because Tom stuck with Slaby through some pretty tough times and had always been reliable and honest with him.

Thinking out loud, Michael said the place to switch the marks back to Thunder would probably be at the mill. Tom would be at the mill anyway and he didn't think anyone would be suspicious if they also brought Sven, maybe Deiter, too. If they tried to re-mark the logs while they were still piled at camp, Jason would likely find out. Michael said he knew some of the guys at the mill. Good men. He had helped them the previous year when they were swamped and short-handed. Michael said he pitched in separating out the high-grade maple used for expensive furniture from the ordinary logs.

"What the hell's holdin' you up, Michael?" John Bundy yelled. "Get your ass on the road."

"I'm on my way, John," Michael called back. Then he looked at me and said, "Thanks, Will. Keep this under your hat. Okay?"

15

During the first week of December, I watched the men load the Thunder Logging and Seely hardwood logs onto rail cars. The pine logs were stacked nearby on top of a slope leading to the river but were being ignored. I asked one of the men why the pine logs weren't being loaded. He told me that pine logs float, so they were sent to the mill on the river after the ice breaks up. Floating down the river was the cheapest way to get them to the mill. The hardwood logs are too heavy and sink.

Fifteen empty rail cars had been left on a single-track spur that abutted the logging trail halfway around my circuit. The logs would be loaded on the cars and taken to the mill any day. Most of the logs I saw had the Seely mark. But if you looked closely you could see parts of the Thunder mark that had not been chipped off or completely covered up by the Seely mark that I saw Jason's men apply. I wrote down the identification numbers painted on the side of the flatbed rail cars with the majority of the mis-marked logs. I gave Michael the list. He was already in one of the company trucks with Tom and Sven ready to drive to the mill. Shortly after Michael left, John Bundy, Jason, and a handful of men from the Seely crew also left for the mill in Eau Claire.

Three days later, Sven and Tom came back with the Seely crew. Tom looked livid when he got out of the truck. He and Sven headed toward the bunkhouse, while the Seely crew headed toward the kitchen hoping to get something to eat. I ran from the barn after Tom and Sven, following them into the bunkhouse where Deiter and a few other Thunder crew were playing cards on a bunk. I hoped they'd think I was invited by someone.

"Hi Tom," Deiter said. Tom kept walking to his bunk on the far end of the room. He threw the small bag he carried onto the bunk, and then sat down next to his bag.

"What happened at the mill, Sven?" Deiter asked.

"Jason screwed us. Tom, Michael, and I watched for our logs in the rail yard at the mill. When we found 'em, we cut the Seely marks off all that maple we cut last fall before Slaby died. Nobody saw us. The mill calculated over eight hundred and thirty thousand board feet with Thunder marks, even without counting those that Jason's men changed that went into the mill before we found 'em. The three of us went to Jason's room at the hotel to show him the mill inventory numbers. Michael wanted to collect on that bet he made with Jason. He was right on the button with his figurin' of at least eight hundred thousand. Jason told us that *we were the ones who cheated.* He said the only way we coulda got over eight hundred thousand feet was if we changed Seely marks! That lyin' son-of-a-bitch said there was no way he was goin' to pay off on that bet or pay our crew for any timber we cut, other than the five hundred thousand feet he's already paid for when he bought the company. I'd of throw'd him right out the window behind him if he hadn't had the sheriff standin' right there in the room. He knew damn well he was cheatin' us and we'd be pissed, so he just paid the sheriff a few bucks and made sure we didn't make any trouble. Michael's still at the mill tryin' to show the sheriff the logs where the old Thunder marks is still clear under the Seely stamp. But there ain't no way that sheriff is gonna see anythin' Jason don't want him to," Sven said.

"Why would he purposely piss us off?" Deiter asked.

Tom looked up for the first time and said, "Because the asshole is tryin' to show us who's the boss. He knows damn well he ain't half as good as his old man, and his old man thinks his kid is a moron. Jason doesn't want to be in the loggin' business. He ain't got the balls for it. So he's lookin' at buyin' cut-over land and sellin' it to Polacks and Croats. All his pin-dick buddies do that and keep tellin' him he should, too. He's already sent Michael to check out swamp and some acres that was cut five years ago. Why would he do that? There ain't no timber on it. By cheatin' us out of that pay, he has extra money to buy that crap land and his old man will never see it on the books. Then he figures he'll sell it at a big profit and show his old man how it's done."

"What we gonna do?" Deiter asked.

"Damned if I know. There's still a lot of loggin' to do so I figure I'll just keep workin' cause I need this job," Tom said.

"As much as I hate to, I'm gonna do the same," Sven said.

16

Two days after Michael arrived back at camp from the mill, I was sitting on Deiter's top bunk watching Michael teach Tom and a few of the men how to play chess. I was trying to learn, too. Jason entered the bunkhouse waving and shouting greetings to some of his crew. Most of his men ignored him. He walked over to the chess game.

"You boys trying to learn a gentleman's game?"

"I am," Tom said coldly.

"What about you, Michael?" Jason asked.

"I am always learning, too."

"Whenever you think you're good enough, let me know and I'll speed your learning along. I made a few bucks playing chess at the Men's Club at college. I'd just love to teach you both a thing or two," Jason said.

Before his words had stopped echoing through the bunkhouse, Tom said, "Michael is good enough now. Why don't you play him?"

Michael said nothing, but stared up at Jason.

"Why not? Somebody's gotta take you down a notch or two. I don't suppose you boys will try to cheat me again with all these fellas watching you." Jason sat down.

"Do you care to make this interesting? Maybe a little bet on the outcome?" Michael said.

"You still owe me a hundred bucks from our last bet and you want to try again?" Tom started to step toward Jason, but must have thought better of it and stayed put.

"Well, okay. Let's make it for the hundred I owe you and five hundred more," Michael said.

"Where the hell do you think you're going to get five hundred bucks from?" Jason asked.

"I'll stake him for it," Tom said.

"You gonna use some of that fifteen percent you got from me buyin' Thunder? Shit, I'll just be winning my own money back. Oh, what the hell. This will be fun! It's a deal. Let's play."

Jason started out the game seeming very self-assured. After seven or eight moves he started taking a lot longer between moves. He turned white when Michael checkmated him two moves later.

"Lucky bastard," Jason muttered when he was finally able to speak.

"Like to play another? I think I just might get lucky again," Michael said.

"I don't have the time to waste on this shit," Jason said, and stood up.

"It doesn't look like another game would take any time at all," Tom said. There were loud hoots and howls from the thirty men from both camps who were watching the exchange. That was the only time I ever saw the entire crew laugh at Jason's expense. It seemed as though the old Thunder crew couldn't wait to show their contempt for Jason.

Jason reached into his pants pocket and withdrew a money clip of folded bills. He peeled off the top five one hundred dollar bills. "Try not to lose that before I can win it back," Jason said, as he handed the money to Michael.

Jason must have remembered what it was that brought him to the bunkhouse in the first place. He interrupted the congratulatory handshakes and back slaps Michael was getting, and said, "Tomorrow early, get your ass over to John Bundy's office and pick up a map to five or six sections I need assessed for standing lumber, and try to be more accurate with your assessment this time. There are two sections along the Chippewa River that Wisconsin Northern

Railroad's sellin' that I'm particularly interested in and need to know what's there. We haven't had that much snow the last couple of days so you shouldn't have a problem on the main roads. They'll get you close. You can snowshoe the last couple of miles," Jason said.

Jason left. In a rare display of camaraderie, members of both crews patted Michael's back and gave him their congratulations. I felt proud that he was my friend.

When things quieted down, Michael motioned to Tom to come with him. I joined them. Once outside, Michael asked Tom, "Do you know where I can safely stash this five hundred bucks? I'm uncomfortable hiding it in my bunk. There are a few *gentlemen* in this crew that wouldn't give a second thought to slitting my throat for that much money."

"Yeah, I think you're probably right. Mattie can keep it in a safe place."

"I don't know, Tom. Are you sure?" Michael asked.

"I trust Mattie as much as anybody in this camp. We go back a ways."

"Let's see what she says," Michael said. We walked to the mess hall.

When Mattie looked up and saw Tom, her whole body smiled. "Tom, you old wood rat, what you and your buddy want, a little somethin' ta eat? That kitchen rule don't apply to you, Tom."

"Not tonight Mattie. But I do need your help."

"Well I can't do much but I'll help if a'kin," Mattie said.

"Michael here needs a place to keep this bag till morning. Can you help him out?"

"Why that's nuthin. I be happy to oblige. You come by before breakfast, else I be too busy to fetch it for ya."

"Thanks, Mattie. I appreciate your help," Michael said.

"Well, I'm happy to help ya."

After they left I said to Mattie, "I thought no one got food except at mealtime."

"That Tom Nelson is special so I treats him special."

"How is he special?" I said.

"We was at a camp near Ashland when I was pregnant with Abraham. I started havin' pains in my back an' right here at the top of my stomach. I was real worried about the baby. I went over to see the camp foreman. He was talkin' to Tom. That foreman looked at me an' said, 'You darkies is tough and you'll be fine in the mornin'.' I'm a strong woman but I could tell I was in real trouble. When that foreman walked back to his quarters I was frettin'. Well, Tom could tell I weren't right and come back an' took me to see a doctor. He used the only truck in camp. We got to town about two in the mornin'. Tom pounded on the doctor's door until finally his wife answered. She was real nice 'til she seen me. I guess she was none too pleased to have to git up in the middle of the night for a darkie. Well, Tom walked right past her and helped me in. He set me down in the doctor's room. I guess that doc heard the commotion and got up. 'Bout an hour later he induced labor and Abraham was born. Weighed less 'an five pounds.

"The doctor told me I had the 'grippe' and if he hadn't induced labor and Abraham weren't delivered, both of us would prob'ly of died. Then the doc said I had to leave and would be okay once I started passin' water again. Tom took me back to his place for a couple days 'til I regained my strength. I couldn't do much to show my 'preciation, so I named Abraham after him. Yup, his middle name is Thomas. Least I kin do is feed Tom Nelson when he's hungry."

Before sunup the next morning, Michael came to the mess hall to pick up his bag. Mattie sat him down with Abraham and me and gave us all biscuits and gravy. After breakfast Michael walked over to John Bundy's office for the map and legal descriptions of the sections Jason asked him to assess.

I finished breakfast and headed to the pump to get water in my bucket and start my rounds. In the yard I ran into Michael as he left Bundy's office. Holding the map Bundy just gave him, Michael, talking to himself as I walked past, said, "I've walked this land before." Then he noticed me crossing his path. "Oh hey, Chickadee, will you let Deiter know that I'm depositing this money in a bank account and will be back in a couple of days? I'll be walking the tract Jason's interested in."

"Sure will." I told Deiter right after I had finished my circuit.

17

As the weeks passed, I became more confident on the trails and couldn't resist the temptation to attempt to slide down the hills in the icy ruts. I would fall periodically, but when I didn't, it was exhilarating. By the end of November, I was able to handle even the steepest slopes with ease. When there were horse apples in the runway, I would step onto the middle portion of the trail where the snow provided enough traction to stop without falling or spilling water.

One morning just before Christmas, I stepped outside to begin my duties. The cold took my breath away. I had never been outside before when it was that cold. It read thirty-eight degrees below zero on the Allis Chalmers thermometer nailed to the side of the barn. I sniffed my runny nose and my nostrils temporarily froze closed. While the frigid air was completely still, sliding down the hills generated enough wind on my face to be painful. I shielded my exposed face with my arm and pulled the collar of my coat up as high as I could. I tried to hurry around the trails, but between stops I repeatedly needed to use my screwdriver to chip a hole in the ice that had formed on the water in my bucket. The water splashed onto my leather mittens and froze them solid, making it difficult to hold the screwdriver and ladle.

I arrived back in record time, the ladle frozen fast in the last two inches of water inside the bucket. My face, fingers, and toes were all numb. When I got inside and stood in front of the stove, the numbness gave way to tingling and then pain, especially on my fingers, cheeks, and the tips of my ears. Mattie saw me and smiled, "It gits a whole lot colder 'an this up here."

Later that afternoon when I was in the barn helping Abraham clean out the chicken boxes, Max came into the barn for some chains. He said, "Hey Chickadee, you got some people pretty damn mad at you, boy, includin' me. You left some turds on the track. The runner hit 'em and the sled turned hard right. The load had some mighty big logs on it. Those heavy suckers busted the chains. One of 'em nearly took my head off. We'll be spendin' the rest of the day tryin' to fix that load. Damn it, kid, you gotta be more careful."

"You got some people pretty damn mad." (Image A201418 from the Forest County Historical Museum)

Nearly every logger I saw that day had words for me. Especially Bundy. I was sure I was in for a beating, but Bundy finally calmed down enough to just warn me that if it ever happened again, he would personally beat me with an axe handle and "throw my scrawny ass out of camp." It never did happen again. Even on the coldest days, I was especially cautious not to miss any rough spots and the trails were clear when I finished.

Deiter tried to ease my obvious embarrassment and the sting of admonishment from the men. Frankly, it was worse than any beating they could have given. Nyka was the only other logger to be supportive, saying in a group loud enough so I could hear, "Remember the last little shit? We had to check the trails every damn day."

In the barn Abraham and I exchanged stories of punishments we'd gotten. Abraham told me of "whoopin's" he'd gotten from a man friend of Mattie's. He had regularly beaten them both until finally Mattie had enough and chased him out with a carving knife. Shortly after, they left the Gogebic mines. That was two years ago. Unlike Abraham I had never been beaten, or even spanked. My stories of being scolded harshly seemed particularly anemic after hearing him tell of his experiences. I changed the subject.

"I want to be a logger, not a Chickadee. I want to be like Deiter," I said.

Abraham shook his head, "Will, that work is jus' too tough fer a kid. You ever try sawin' or choppin on maple logs?"

"Not yet. But I will and I'm gonna be damn good at it, too!" Abraham didn't answer.

"Some of the loggers have been nice to me," I said.

"Ya? Like who?"

"Well, my friend Deiter for one, and even Nyka."

"Nyka!? Ya be careful around that ol' boy, he ain't what he seems to be," Abraham said.

"What do you mean?"

Just then the side barn door squeaked opened and Nyka strode over to us.

"What you boys talkin' 'bout in here?" Nyka asked. "I'd swear I just heard my name spoke."

"I was just telling Abraham here that you were one of the only loggers that's been nice to me, that's all," I said.

"You ever try sawin' or choppin' a maple?" *(From the collection of the German Settlement History Inc., Ogema, WI)*

Nyka looked suspiciously at us both, but a barely discernible nod by Abraham must have convinced Nyka that was the case, and he burst into a smile and rubbed my hair. "I'm glad that's what you think, boy. Fact is, I come by to give ya a piece of chocolate I won playin' cards yesterday. Seems Tauno Larson took it off a dresser of a whore in town las' Saturday. Tried to bluff me with a pair of fours. He was bettin' this here 'cause after that ol' whore and a whole lot a drinkin', he was outta money," Nyka laughed. "I tried some, but chewin' chaw all day, most stuff don't have much taste. So's you ain't had a very good day and I figured you might like it."

He handed the paper-wrapped candy to me and left.

"See what I mean?" I said.

"Like I say, you be careful of that un'."

I remembered the odd way Michael looked at Nyka the first day I arrived in camp. Mattie warned me about him, too, and now Abraham was telling me to be cautious. But the fact of the matter was that Nyka was nice to me and until that changed, I liked him.

We split the chocolate—ate it slowly and savored it. The last time I had eaten anything sweet was a few weeks before when Mattie treated Abraham and me with "poor man's ice cream," as she called it. After filling two coffee cups with snow, she poured maple syrup over the top. Abraham and I ate it with spoons at the small table in the kitchen. It was delicious. Even now when I get a craving for sweets, that's what I think about.

18

Sunday was our day off. But on the Sunday morning after Nyka stopped by the barn, I decided to get up at my usual time, and with the men still asleep, begin my effort to prove Abraham wrong and become a logger. It was the first Sunday after New Years, 1921.

I knew I needed a lot of practice and had to get stronger. Since I had used an axe to help trim branches from felled trees, I decided to try the two-man saw to see if it would be easier. There was one leaning on the outhouse. Taking it into the woods just far enough so I couldn't be seen from camp, I tried my damnedest to saw through a log. The best I could do was cut a groove an inch deep. The friction of the blade on the sides of the groove and the sap collecting on the blade was too much for me to overcome. I couldn't coax another stroke out of that saw. Alternating between the saw and axe became my training ritual every Sunday morning after that, and I would join the men in the woods to trim branches every day. When the men saw me the first few times, they joked and teased. Max would yell to everyone's delight but mine, "I see a lot of choppin' over there but I sure don't see any chips a flyin'."

It didn't matter to me. I didn't want to be a Chickadee one day longer than I had to. Although the men didn't notice, after a few weeks I could tell I was getting more proficient. Not good, just better than I was.

After I exhausted myself from chopping, one Sunday

morning I decided to explore an area along the river with towering hemlocks and cedar trees well east of any trails I had been on before. Although the crew hadn't begun logging in this part of the woods, I was surprised to see several sets of boot prints.

I followed the trail of prints through the snow along the river for nearly half a mile. In a small clearing surrounded by blackberry bushes I found a strange-looking contraption. It consisted of two 100-gallon oil drums with a large covered vat on top. Near the bottom of each can was a one-foot square hole cut in the side revealing a wood fire. A long coil of copper tubing running parallel to the ground was attached at one end to the top of the vat. From the coil's other end, a clear liquid dripped through a small hole in the lid of a covered wooden barrel. I figured it was maple syrup after overhearing Mattie talking with a local man about getting some syrup for the kitchen. I let the liquid drip on my fingers then eagerly put them in my mouth expecting the familiar sweet taste of syrup.

I couldn't spit the fiery fluid out quickly enough. It burned my throat and tasted awful, but vaguely familiar. Years earlier when my father and mother had friends over just before Father was drafted, I got up first that morning. One of the glasses left on the table from the night before still had some liquid in it, so I sampled it. It burned the same way this liquid did. It was liquor. I wiped my mouth on my sleeve and thought I heard a soft crunch like a footstep in the snow behind me. When I turned around I was looking into the barrel of a rifle. Behind it was a stern-looking man with a boy about my age peeking around from behind him. "Yer a trespassin' an' I shoot trespassers," he said.

"I'm not trespassin'. I was just following the trail and it led me here."

"See, I told you, son, we needed to cover that trail better," the man said over his shoulder. "Whatcha doin' out here in the middle of nowheres then?" the man asked.

"This isn't the middle of nowhere. It's just half a mile from the end of the logging trails," I said.

"You from the loggin' camp, kid?"

"Sure am. I'm the Chick ... I take care of the horses."

"Ya' know curiosity kil't the cat, don't ya, kid?"

The boy, dragging a toboggan, walked out from behind the man and said, "You won't be tellin' any dry agents about us, will ya, kid?"

"I won't tell anyone, I swear," and saw the first positive sign that I just might live through this.

"Well, with you loggers only half mile away, we'd best be movin' the still to another spot anyways." The boy nodded his head in agreement.

"What's your name, kid?"

"Will."

"Well, I'm Frank and this is my boy, Alonzo. We calls 'em Al an' that's all you need to know 'bout us."

"Why are you making liquor out here in the woods and not at home?" I asked.

"Ain't ya heard a Pro'bition, kid?"

"I've heard of it, but I'm not sure what it means."

"It ain't legal to make or sell booze anymore. Tha's what it means."

"This here is moonshine."

"Now I ain't sayin' no more," the man said. "Now we gonna let you go this time, but if I ever sees you anywhere near one of our stills, I'll shoot you right dead, you understan' that, kid?"

"I won't come near it, I swear I won't." I meant what I said.

"Now we're gonna get to tearin' this here still down and move it across the river. Are the loggers gonna cross the river yet this year?"

"No. There's plenty of timber where we're logging now," I said.

"Good, then we should be okay over there a spell."

"Can I help you?" I asked, surprising myself.

After eyeing me a moment, Frank answered mostly thinking out loud, "Well I s'pose another pair a hands won't hurt
an' as long as you don't say nuthin'. You won't know where
we're goin', so sure, you kin give us a hand."

Al and I worked together, doing as Frank directed. The
barrel was half full with moonshine and too heavy for Al and
me to move. After Frank put a cork in the hole on the lid, the
three of us put the barrel on its side and rolled it onto the
toboggan and stood it up.

Despite his father's warning, Al talked the whole time
saying that in addition to moonshining, he and his dad
trapped mink and muskrats along the rivers and area lakes.
They sold the moonshine and pelts in town.

Al told me all about their business and the thirteen other
kids in his family. Seven were younger and six older than
him. Only three boys in the whole brood. The two oldest
boys moved to Superior and worked at the port there. The
girls had no interest in trapping or moonshining, but with
all those mouths to feed, Frank needed to do whatever he
could to make money, and Prohibition was a windfall. He
could get potatoes for next to nothing. It was one of the few
crops that would grow well in the silt and clay soil between
the stones and boulders littering every field. Now, instead
of just brewing a little liquor for himself, Frank was able to
make fifty or sixty dollars a week selling moonshine.

Al said his father knew that this could come to an end at
any time but intended to take advantage of the opportunity
while it lasted. He also complained that he was getting too
old to handle the physical demands of moonshining, and
the Feds were a constant threat. If he could stay out of the
way and operate small-time, his father hoped he would be
of little interest to the feds. He also needed to be sure he
wasn't competing with any of the organized syndicates. But
they tended to stay in cities where they could really make
money by selling booze they bought from moonshiners and
diluting it. But a lot of booze was smuggled in from Canada
through Superior.

I helped the pair drag the toboggan piled with the disassembled pieces of the still the half-mile back to the point where their trail had started, next to the river. Frank pulled aside a large brush pile and revealed a rowboat. They were careful to hide it when they had arrived.

Al said, "Hey Pa, kin I ask Will to come a trappin' with us next week? We kin always use another set a hands skinnin' 'rats."

"S'pose so, if the boy wants to."

"I'd like to," I said.

"Okay then, we'll come by and pick ya up 'round eight next Sunday mornin'. That'll give me a reason to see your camp and where you're loggin' first hand."

We bid goodbyes and the two rowed hard against the current in one of the few sections on the river that remained free of ice.

I couldn't wait to tell Abraham of my adventure, but before I got back, thought better of it. The menacing look on Frank's face was clearly intimidating, and although he became friendlier, I intended to keep my promise and not say anything to anyone. But I thought it was okay when I told Abraham about meeting a boy in the woods playing near the river. Abraham surprised me when he said, "I bet that's the moonshiner's kid."

It turned out that the moonshining operation was a very poorly kept secret. I later found out that it was common knowledge that most of the booze the loggers drank at the bars and whorehouses in town was local brew, all illegal, most of it Frank's. Abraham told me that he heard that Frank Mattson gave the sheriff two quarts a week as insurance so he wouldn't find the stills or harass Frank when he was making deliveries.

19

The first thing I did every morning after breakfast was go to the outhouse. I used it of course, but before I did I would carefully check around the seat and on the floor for coins. Seems the loggers didn't trust each other very much. Whenever nature called at night they'd gather up their money and maybe a prized pocketknife or timepiece and put it in their coat or pants pocket before heading to the outhouse. Half asleep, in the dark, and dropping their trousers often resulted in loose change falling out unnoticed. This was especially true on Saturday nights when the men were liquored up. At first I was tentative about this treasure hunting, but rationalized that there was no way to determine who the owners were. If I wasn't there first, someone else would eventually find it and keep it. Why not me? That Sunday was no exception. As soon as it was light enough to see, I went to the outhouse. That morning I found one dollar and forty-one cents. With the addition of that day's find, my hoard was nearly up to thirty dollars. I kept the money rolled up in a sock tucked under my mattress in the room behind the kitchen. I wasn't sure what I was going to do with the money, but Mother taught me the value of having some money saved for emergencies.

Being Sunday morning, the camp was quiet. The men were still sleeping off Saturday night hangovers. I went out into the woods to trim branches as I usually did on Sundays.

I was just walking back into camp about two hours later

when I saw an old truck bump down the snow-covered dirt road leading into camp. I couldn't tell if it was the Mattson's or Bundy the foreman. As I waited, I imagined what it would be like to be the foreman of my own logging company. Not a Chickadee but a real logger the others respected. Maybe like Sven, but more like Michael or Tom. A slamming truck door interrupted my thoughts.

As I walked toward the truck I noticed Abraham coming out of the barn.

"Hi Will, hi Abraham," Alonzo said. "You wanna come along trappin', Abraham?"

"Nah, can't, got too much ta do in da barn."

I felt a tinge of remorse, remembering that Sunday was my favorite day in the barn. It was the horses' day off, too, and the only day I could spend any time with them.

Frank walked around the yard and asked me how the trails were situated. He knew where the railroad spur and log slides on the river were, so the little information he got fleshed out his understanding of the logging area. After Frank finished his quick look around the camp, we set out to check the traps.

As we drove, Frank described trapping as the best available work to make some money in the dead of winter to supplement his moonshining business. Al spoke like he was on his way to a treasure hunt and clearly enjoyed it. He said that even though they were specifically trapping for mink and muskrats, they never knew what fur bearers they might catch or how many.

For me this was an adventure, a chance to be with someone my own age, and learn something about the area outside of the camp. Abraham was good company, but he didn't like to leave the barn much and didn't like trying anything new.

The Mattsons set their traps along the roads near their home and on the trail to the still. There was a pattern. Every time the road crossed a creek, ditch, or river, they set traps in the open water or under the ice, after they chopped a hole. Each site was baited with an apple slice for muskrats or they just put a trap where they thought an animal would likely go. For mink, they would use muskrat meat or chicken heads for bait. Available sticks were used to make two walls, usually in an inlet along the riverbank, leaving a five- or six-inch opening on one end and the bait up against the bank on the other. In the opening they would set a trap or wire snare. Frank gave a running monologue about what he was doing at each trap setting. I didn't know if it was because I was there or if he just thought it was important for Alonzo to learn.

"Mink like to jus' meander along. They sniff every nook and cranny, over and under every log along the bank," he said. "Good thing ya don't have to use bait every time or we'd be outta chick heads after the second creek." Frank thought his comment was funny and laughed. "Jus' look for a log or hole or somethin' a mink might think is interestin' and set a trap. If a mink comes through you'll git 'em."

I helped whenever I was instructed to do something, which wasn't often. They didn't want extra scent or sign left at the trap sites to spook the critters. Frank showed me where to walk and stand while he and Al did their work.

When Al brought a one-inch diameter stick to build a small barrier, Frank gave it back to him and told him to find one smaller. "Ya only need enough of a twig to be in their way to make 'em swim one way or the other. Smaller's better, looks more natural. Even a black bear 'ill step himself around a lil' saplin' no bigger 'n your pinkie."

After seeing a few of the muskrats being harvested I thought it looked cruel. "Don't the traps hurt the animals?" I asked.

"I s'pose it does," Frank said. "There ain't no good way to kill somethin'. Nature ain't too gentle neither. Rats either get eaten by a mink or starve when the water level drops too far in the winter. At least when we kill 'em we make a few bucks."

Most muskrats and mink they caught that day had already drowned by the time we arrived. The trap on their leg weighed them down and kept them under water. Those that didn't drown or were trapped on land and still alive, were rapped on the back of their neck with a small wooden club, "so's not to tear the pelt or cause too much bleedin'," according to Frank. Al carried a backpack with the club, bait, traps, and a second sack for the carcasses. "Don't want the traps smellin' like dead critter," Frank explained. Frank carried the .22 rifle that had been pointed at my nose the week before. He said he kept it with him to shoot any grouse or hares they might spook and uses a .22, "cause the little woman don't like pluckin' birdshot, but for me to git 'em with this here pea shooter, they gotta be standin' mighty still."

Most of their traps were set on the edge of the fast-moving water entering and exiting culverts and flowing under small bridges because they tended to stay open during the cold spells. They also set traps along the trail to their still since they needed to walk there every day anyway. Snares were typically set for snowshoe hare; fox and coyote were caught with leg-hold traps. We reached the end of the trap line and arrived at the new site of their still. They had eight musk-rats, two mink, a raccoon, five hares, and a gray fox.

"How much can you sell these for?" I asked.

"A prime 'rat fetches about two bits, the mink three bucks, the 'coon, a buck and a quarter, and two or three bucks for the fox. The snowshoes ain't hardly worth the effort. Their skin tears too easy and you only get a dime tops," Frank said.

After sorting through their catch, Frank said, "We made ourselves ten or twelve bucks. Not bad for a mornin's work, hey? How 'bout you take them hares, Will? There's so many this year that I'm gettin' a little tired of eatin' 'em. Al, help clean 'em up for him."

While Frank tended the still, we skinned and gutted the hares. I followed Al's example, trying not to show how disagreeable I thought the job was. Each of the skins Al pulled off the carcass was intact. Mine were in pieces from where I inadvertently pushed my fingers through the pelt, pulled too hard, or cut through with a knife. Al packed up the hares in a gunny sack and we joined Frank at the truck for the two-mile ride back to camp. Ordinarily they would have walked, but Frank was going to run some moonshine into town and suggested that they drop me off on the way.

Mattie was delighted when she saw the hares. "Why they's big 'uns" she said, as she removed the carcasses from the sack. "Where'd ya get 'em?"

"The moonshiners took me trapping with them."

"What ya think we outta do with 'em?" Mattie asked. "I kin cut 'em in pieces over rice, or maybe hasenpfeffer, you bein' German an' all."

I picked rice. Mattie went back to the huge dough oval she had been rolling out.

"What are ya makin' for tonight, Mattie?" I asked.

"Pasties."

She told me how she learned to make them when she cooked for the copper miners. Pasties were the ideal lunch because they would easily fit in a coat pocket. "Since they stayed in them mine shafts durin' their entire shift, they needed somethin' that wouldn't spill or crumble. They could jus' blow the dust off and take 'em out of the newspaper they was wrapped in. They's fillin' too," she said.

There were a lot of Finns, Slavs, Swedes, and Germans working the copper mines and they were all very particular about how they liked their pasties. Mattie said she experimented until she found a pasty that most of the men liked. The most important thing was baking them with a dab of lard on top to ensure the pasties browned and crusted up, keeping the contents sealed.

Mattie served the hares that evening. She cut each into eight pieces, cooked it in gravy, and poured it over wild rice. I was disappointed that the men griped about the meager portion of meat. Mattie reminded them that she was already out of venison from last fall, except for some scrapple, and the only butchered hog was still hanging in the smokehouse. She said she was saving the fifteen pounds of bacon that hung curing in my room and that they should be grateful for the hares.

"Rat fetches about two bits." *(Image BK042 from the collection of the German Settlement History Inc., Ogema, WI)*

20

Dinners at logging camps weren't fancy. Biscuits, mounds of potatoes, beans, cabbage, squash, chicken, roast pork, venison, blood sausage, pasties, stew, and wild rice bought from local Indians harvesting near the Totagetic were the staples from Mattie's kitchen. The men sat and Mattie and Abraham brought the platters and bowls heaped high with food and put them on the tables. Once seated, every diner simultaneously grabbed, scooped, passed, or tossed food in a short-lived frenzy until each had a satisfactory portion on his plate.

After the initial chaos, things quieted while the ravenous group ate. As they ate, Mattie circled the group refilling empty bowls if she had more, or collecting the empty dishes to be put in the hot soapy water waiting in the washing tubs next to the stove. Abraham washed the dishes and I dried. Only on special occasions like Christmas would Mattie make rice pudding or sugar cookies for dessert.

For breakfast Mattie would make scrambled eggs, biscuits and gravy from the night before, and plenty of bread. From the first day, I loved the smell of the kitchen, especially when Mattie baked bread.

One evening I heard a shout in the mess hall and walked from my room to the kitchen door to investigate. One of the few advantages of being a Chickadee was that other than the bunkhouse, no one paid me any mind, or noticed or cared much if I was hanging around. A Chickadee was just sort of invisible and I learned to use that to my advantage.

Mattie had spilled baked beans on Nyka. Sven, the giant Swede, had turned in his seat and bumped her arm as she was putting the beans on the table. "Shit! Be careful with them goddamn beans, you whore!" Nyka yelled.

"I don' care what ya say 'bout me," Mattie shot back, "but don't you blaspheme my beans."

Some of the men recognized Mattie's attempt to defuse the situation and laughed. Nyka would have none of it. He picked up a bread knife and started to stand. Mattie grabbed his wrist and for an instant there was a stalemate. But Nyka was not ready to let it die and tried to wrest his hand free. I guess twenty years of kneading dough gave Mattie powerful hands and with her girth, she leaned forward and down on Nyka's arm, pinning it to the table. Despite his strength, Nyka couldn't pull his arm out of her grip. In that awkward, painful position there was no way he was going to move Mattie. I could see the long, white scar on Nyka's arm where the bandage had been when I first met him.

Most men would have yielded when their steam burned off, but not Nyka. He struggled and pulled until Tom and Sven came to Mattie's aid. The two men held Nyka. With Sven intervening, Mattie let go of Nyka's arm and went on with her duties as though nothing had happened.

Sven had inadvertently started the whole affair. He occupied so much space it was not surprising that he was the one to bump into her. He was the biggest man I had ever seen. Not only was he tall, standing six-foot-eight, but he filled the entire doorway when he entered a room. Sven's exhibitions of strength were legendary among the loggers and even Nyka was not about to challenge him.

Nyka finally settled down after being restrained and getting a stern look from Sven. Nyka uttered a few more curses under his breath and resumed his meal. I was still in the kitchen doorway directly behind Nyka and heard Sven lean over and whisper to him, "Anythin' happen to that lady, *anythin'*, I'm goin' to make ya wish it hadn't." Nyka didn't fear anyone, but he must have taken the threat from Sven seriously, because the matter never came up again. Tempers often flared, but Nyka's reaction over such a minor issue made me more attentive to the warnings I had heard about him from others.

21

L ater that week Al walked the two miles over to the lumber camp to visit. I was busy with Abraham in the barn but happy to see my friend and invited him in while I did chores with Abraham. Al pitched in with the barn chores and we talked. He came by to see if I wanted to help make a special delivery into town on Saturday. It took me a second to figure out that he was talking about their moonshine delivery. I accepted. I liked going into town but had only been there twice before with Mattie and Abraham to pick up supplies.

As promised, on Saturday afternoon Al and his father arrived at the camp to pick me up. The loggers were just beginning to wander in from the woods. Those that were single or living away from home were eager to get ready for their Saturday night on the town. The local workers with families usually headed home evenings, including Saturdays. Most walked. Max, the teamster, had the longest walk of anyone, nearly four miles one way. Tom and a handful of others could afford to drive trucks.

I looked into the back of the truck as I climbed into the passenger's side behind Al. Behind the seat in the bed of the truck were a pile of furs and eight crates of potatoes with bales of hay packed in between. Frank's first stop was at the hardware and feed store at the edge of town to sell about a month's worth of stretched and dried pelts. Inside, Frank and the fur buyer carefully examined each pelt. After looking at each one, the buyer carefully recorded numbers in a column on a piece of brown paper using a stub of a pencil. After the final tally he looked up and told Frank, "I'll give ya ninety-three dollars and fifty-five cents for the whole lot."

Frank looked pleased and asked, "Ya sure? I figured them pelts to be sixty-eight bucks, seventy-five tops."

"People want mink collars and coats," the buyer said. "I can sell every mink ya can catch. The furriers I sell to are buyin' every pelt they see. Can't keep up with the demand."

Frank took the money and said, "We'll be tryin' to fill that demand best we can. Ain't that right, boys? I don't think your momma will complain too much if we go celebrate a little. Maybe we can stop over to the drugstore after our deliveries."

With the pelts sold, Frank began the deliveries to the brothels and backroom bars. Frank, Al, and I each carried a crate with bottles of moonshine laid at the bottom with potatoes piled on top to conceal the illegal booze.

I asked Frank, "Why do you pile potatoes on top of the liquor? Doesn't everyone already know what you're delivering?"

"The sheriff makes us do it. He's gotta claim he don't know what the hell we're doin' when them local teetotalers get all up in arms. I s'pose there's still some folks in town who actually don't know what we're up to. So's I give the sheriff a couple a quarts a week to keep him from lookin' under them taters," Frank said.

We walked to Margie's with our next delivery. When we first entered I must have blushed when I realized we were in a whorehouse. We passed the scantily clad "welcomers" who were congregating in the parlor around an overstuffed sofa and clashing love seat. The girls giggled as Alonzo and I walked by. One of them blocked my way, playfully took my face in both her hands and kissed my forehead, "You all come back here to visit me when you're a little older, you hear," she said. Frank overheard and turned around and said, "Hey, them's Christian boys. Ya don't be puttin' any kinda thoughts in their heads."

"You all come back now." *(LegendsofAmerica.com)*

Frank's warning came too late. The thoughts were there. Twenty-three years later, I still remember the smell of that cheap perfume.

We walked past the eight or ten tables and chairs in the barroom and up to a huge oak bar against the back wall. At the bar, Frank put his case with eight quart bottles on the bar and unloaded it. He did the same with the four quarts in the cases Al and I carried. Leaving the bottles on the bar, Frank put the cases on the floor. An older lady walked out from a room behind the bar. "Hi, Margie!" Frank said. "You think sixteen quarts will be enough?"

Compared to the provocative dress of the girls in the parlor, Margie looked more like an aging school teacher or seamstress than a madam. Her hair was piled on top of her head and her dress had a high collar, long sleeves, and went down to the floor.

"Sixteen should do it. I have a few left from last week," she said. "Still two bucks a bottle?"

"Yup."

She paid Frank and we turned to walk the gauntlet, passing by the girls on our way out. I looked at the floor and walked quickly, probably red as hell.

After two more deliveries, Frank led us to the drugstore on Board Street. At the counter Frank asked for three Coca Colas and placed fifteen cents on the counter. The clerk produced three eight-ounce bottles and pried off the caps using an opener attached to the counter. Frank handed one to Al and the other to me and said, "Thanks for helpin' us with the *potato* delivery, Will."

We each carried our bottle to a table by the window, took a seat and watched the men from the various logging camps arrive in town to spend their money—some of it on the moonshine we just delivered.

I had never had a Coca Cola before and took a big swig. Damn that was good! It tickled my nose on the way down and produced a man-sized burrrrp on the way up, generating laughter from everyone within earshot. Embarrassed, I took smaller sips and let the carbonation play in my mouth. I savored every drop in that bottle.

I tried to keep from thinking about the encounter at Margie's, and instead focused on my outhouse enterprise. Sunday mornings were the best for finding coins and I anticipated that the next morning would be particularly good. Most of the men had gotten paid on Friday.

Looking out the window from our table I saw a man walk out from an alley next to the drugstore. It was Nyka. I recognized him immediately and watched him cross the street and enter the barbershop. I assumed he was headed to the upstairs bar where we made a delivery earlier.

"Well boys, it's seven-thirty, we don't want the missus worryin' too much. Let's git a'goin'," Frank said.

After Frank drove me back to camp, I told Mattie and Abraham about my trip to town and my tasty first Coca Cola. Early the next morning, I went to the outhouse to relieve myself and to check for loose change. Just as I had hoped, there were a few coins lying on the floor. It wasn't until I stepped outside that I noticed one of the coins was a five dollar gold piece. What a find! That was going to be my lucky day!

After breakfast I heard some loud talking and wandered outside for a better look. It was the sheriff from town questioning the loggers about a girl that had been assaulted in town. Some of the men had heard about the girl being hurt, but most knew nothing of it. The sheriff was interested in questioning the men who were at Margie's the previous night, but showed particular interest in talking with Nyka. I stood behind the men who gathered to hear the proceedings. The sheriff asked Nyka where he had been last night. Nyka laughed and said he hoped the officer could help him answer the question.

The officer wasn't amused. He glared at Nyka and said, "I'm asking you."

Nyka's face darkened and he took a step toward the officer. "You asked, I answered."

The officer didn't reach for his gun, but he didn't back away either. Max broke the momentary standoff and said, "You was with us at Margie's when we got to town. Didn't you accompany that Dutch girl to her room?"

Tauno Larson said, "Yup, that's right."

Some of the men who were there with them nodded.

"I sure was there with the boys, but can't tell you right off which girl I ..." Nyka paused and looked at the men, "*visited* with," he said.

There were snickers over his word choice.

"Well, it was that Dutch girl that got the hell beat outta her," the officer said. "She told me that one of you boys went back to her room after doing your business and got real mad at her. She had no idea why, but whoever it was punched her so hard it broke her cheekbone and two ribs when she hit the wall. She's hurt real bad."

"It was that Dutch girl you went with, Nyka," Tauno reiterated, oblivious to Nyka's irritation.

"Could'a been, I just can't say for sure," Nyka said. "But the girl I left was praisin' the glory of my visit when I left that room." Prompting a few more snickers, "She was jus' fine and dandy."

"What time did all this happen, officer?" Max asked.

"Sometime around seven-thirty last night," the officer said.

"Well, I was at the barbershop at seven last night, prob'ly before that," Nyka said.

I knew that wasn't true. I remembered exactly what time it was when Nyka walked past the drugstore. We had finished our Cokes when Frank said that it was seven-thirty and that we'd better get goin' before Alonzo's momma started worryin'.

I was about to interject that information but was too far back and thought better of a Chickadee butting into men's business.

Later I was talking with Abraham in the barn and told him about what the sheriff said and what I saw.

"It had ta be Nyka," he said.

"How do you know that, you weren't there?"

"There's only one man in this here camp that's crazy that way and that's Nyka."

I knew Nyka was wrong about the times, but that didn't necessarily make him guilty. He was my friend after all.

Later that Sunday, Nyka came to the barn. "Abraham, you in here?" he shouted. I was putting oats in the feed bags for Max to take on the wagon for the horses in the morning. "Nope," I answered, "only me." I walked out so Nyka could see for himself who it was. "Chickadee, hey, I need a small piece of leather to fix this here split in my boot. Damn axe glanced off a' oak branch I was trimmin' and chopped a slice inta' my boot." Nyka pointed down to his left boot where I could see a two-inch gash splitting the top and right through the sole of the boot.

"Did it cut your foot?"

"Na, axe went right t'ween ma toes," Nyka said.

I got a piece of leather that Max used to patch harnesses and handed it to Nyka. "Get me a piece 'a balin' wire too," Nyka said, "I'll wire the sole together so's it don't split more. I been walkin' around for two days with a wet foot and I gotta do somthin'."

Nyka took off his boot and pulled out the old newspaper he had pushed into the toe as a makeshift repair. Then he held up the boot and took a good look at the hole. Gauging the size of the patch he needed, Nyka began working on the leather. He was struggling to cut the leather evenly. I moved closer to help and smelled something familiar ... moonshine! It was heavy on Nyka's breath. He was drunk, even though he seemed fine earlier when he spoke with the sheriff.

John Bundy absolutely prohibited any liquor in camp. Maybe Nyka had found Mattson's still. Two weeks earlier Frank moved it back to the south side of the river near where it had been when I first stumbled onto it. Frank moved his stills periodically, just so no one could say for certain where they were at any given time. At the drugstore Frank had told Al and me about a couple of boys near Hurly who were arrested for bootlegging. They had carelessly left their still in the same spot and the feds found it.

I figured Nyka must have found Frank's still. Mattson would be mad when he discovered his moonshine was being pilfered. Although I didn't know it then, Mattson was already aware of the theft and the damage to the still. He'd be determined to find the culprit.

I knew better than to suggest cutting the leather for

Nyka and just watched. Nyka broke the silence. "I hope that dumbfuck of a cop don't think I had anythin' to do with that whore gettin' whooped. I recall bein' over at the barber's drinkin' with da boys when all the commotion was s'posed ta be happenin'."

I didn't know if Nyka had lied to the officer and was lying to me, or if he was just confused about the time. I still trusted him and gave him the benefit of the doubt.

Trying to help him recall the events better, I said, "Actually you weren't at the barbershop at seven. Nope. It was real close to seven-thirty." Nyka looked at me with a frightening, piercing stare.

"What makes ya think ya have any idea when I was there?"

"Because I was in the drugstore with the Mattsons when Frank said we'd better get goin' because it was seven-thirty. That's when I saw you walk from the side of the drugstore over to the barbershop."

Nyka didn't say anything else while he finished the repair to his boot. He tried to fit the leather patch over the hole. It didn't fit. Nyka tossed the patch on the floor, then used his pocketknife to punch a line of small holes along each side of the gash in the toe of his boot. He stood up, looked around and walked over to a stack of hay bales. He pulled a pliers out of his coat pocket and snipped through the wire that had been holding one of the bales together. The wire popped apart. Nyka grabbed one end and snipped five or six small pieces from the baling wire. He sat down, bent the wire pieces into a U-shape and pushed the wire up with one point through the hole he punched on each side of the gash. Once each wire piece was in place, Nyka used the pliers to twist together the ends of the wires protruding through the toe of his boot. After a quick examination of his work he declared the job finished and put the boot back on.

Once it was laced up and secure, he took a last look at the repair, kicked and stomped it on the ground to be sure it would hold, and then turned his attention to me. "I'd like to show ya somthin' pretty interestin'."

"What is it?"

"Oh jus' somthin' you oughta see."

"I've got a lot of work to do here."

"You jus' forget 'bout any shit ya gotta do in da' barn. We can take care of it later. Come on, let's go."

I was apprehensive about Nyka's ambiguity, the fact that he had been drinking, and my growing skepticism about our friendship. I debated with myself the wisdom of going with Nyka but got my coat on and walked with the man toward the trails I knew better than anyone. When I saw the direction we were headed, I figured that Nyka was going to show me Mattson's still. That had to be it. Well, there was no harm in that. I could feign surprise and then tell the Mattsons that Nyka found their still the next time I saw them.

Nyka walked down the center of the trail, I slid and walked on the icy sled rails just as we had done the first day I arrived at camp. This time however, I was sure-footed, and at the first slope showed off a little. I slid down the rail with perfect balance and confidence I had gained from months of daily circuits around those trails.

I waited at the bottom for Nyka to amble down the center snow-covered strip between the rails. When he reached the bottom I could see that he was not impressed. In fact, he appeared downright annoyed. "Don't do that ag'in," he said, taking hold of my coat sleeve. The loss of what control I had of the situation alarmed me.

I asked Nyka again, "Where're we going? What do you want to show me?"

This time having control of me, Nyka answered my question. "I thought it was jus' 'bout time you saw where the last Chickadee went off to." It was at that point that I realized I had made a huge mistake coming with him. He was scaring the hell out of me!

I had thought about Chester many times and wondered where he went or what happened to him. How could Nyka know?

"He just ran away, didn't he?"

"Well I guess you'll jus' have ta see," Nyka answered.

"I don't want to."

"Don' matter what you want."

Near the top of another slope in the trail, I felt Nyka's grip on my sleeve ease. I decided that trying to escape was worth the risk and this might be the best chance I would get.

I mustered all my strength, yanked my arm as hard as I could and dislodged it from Nyka's grip. Using the traction of the snow-covered portion of the trail as leverage, I threw my body forward onto the icy rail before Nyka could recover his hold.

I slid ahead of Nyka just as I had done earlier. As he chased me down the trail he lost his footing and tripped. He was no match for me on the icy path. I came to another slope and knew I would extend my lead and ensure that I would beat Nyka back to camp where I could alert Michael or Tom or Mattie, whoever I could find first. I hoped it would be Sven.

Halfway down the slope I looked over my shoulder to see where Nyka was. I didn't see the frozen clump on the trail ahead. My foot hit it and I tumbled headfirst down the remainder of the slope. Dazed for an instant, I got up slowly but ready to continue my escape. Nyka was able to make up some ground. When I fell he stopped and picked up a sturdy limb from the side of the trail, which was littered with branches hewn from the felled trees. I heard him snap off the branching end over his knee. He tossed that part away and kept the heavy three-foot bottom section. I got up, struggled to regain my footing, but kept an eye on Nyka. Using a side-arm throwing motion, Nyka sent the sturdy branch spiraling down the center of the trail a few feet off the ground. Before I could make my getaway, the branch caught me behind my knees, knocked me down, and bruised the backs of both legs. This time I could not recover quickly enough and Nyka was soon over me.

He dragged me by the coat collar off the trail and into the woods. "You ain't gonna pull that ag'in," Nyka sneered, as he huffed from exertion. About two hundred yards off the trail in an un-logged area and not far from the original Mattson still site, Nyka tossed me onto a windfall log. It struck me hard in the stomach. I turned around and looked at Nyka. He stepped back a couple of feet and he kicked the snow from a small mound, revealing what looked like discarded laundry.

The more snow Nyka kicked away the clearer it became that it was a small body. I gasped when I realized I was staring into the hollow eye socket of a skull. The top of the skull was covered by a red knit hat. Nyka brushed away more snow and leaves, and revealed a small skeletal hand that rested on a rusted knife. It appeared that the skull was looking along the partially covered coat sleeve and right at the knife.

Nyka followed my gaze to the rusted knife. "Tha's why I gave you that stubby lil' screwdriver for your Chickadeean. This one took a swipe at me with that knife and cut me real good on my arm," he said and pointed to his scar. "Guess I oughta make introductions," Nyka laughed. "Chickadee meet the last Chickadee."

Nyka reached for his belt. "Now boy, I want ya ta do jus' as I tell ya. You jus' go ahead and drop yer pants and lean over that windfall behind ya."

Things suddenly seemed to be in slow motion, it was like a dream. How could this be happening? Without any idea of what to do, I turned to comply, numbed by the hopelessness of the situation. I remember thinking that at least I would be rid of my nightmares—and dead, maybe I would see Mother again.

A loud crack broke the silence and I snapped my head around to investigate. Nyka had a strange look on his face and turned his head to look over his shoulder. I saw blood on the side of his face.

About twenty yards away stood Frank Mattson. He was bolting another cartridge into his .22 rifle. Nyka spun and charged at Mattson. I saw red flecks of Nyka's blood dot the snow as he ran. Mattson's first shot hit Nyka at the top of his right shoulder. The bullet must have struck his cheek when it exited out the front.

Nyka had run less than ten feet before Mattson's second shot hit him in the right breast. Even being hit a second time didn't slow Nyka's charge. Mattson was still chambering his third cartridge when Nyka tackled him hard to the ground. The two men struggled but despite his wounds, Nyka's rage and enormous strength gave him the upper hand. Nyka used his forearm as a club and repeatedly struck Mattson on the side of the head while sitting on top of him. Nyka pulled the gun from Frank's hands and stood up. From behind him I could see him position the gun against his hip for leverage to compensate for the unresponsiveness of his right arm. He aimed the gun at Mattson's forehead. Mattson remained motionless on the ground looking at Nyka with an expression of a man expecting to die.

He was probably surprised instead to watch Nyka's head turn upward as though he were casually looking for a bird in a tree, then fall face down on the ground, nearly landing on Mattson. A rusted knife handle was sticking out of the middle of Nyka's back.

"You okay Mr. Mattson?" I asked, standing where Nyka had just been.

"I believe I am. Can't believe I jus' winged that son-of-a-bitch." Mattson stood up holding his jaw. "I 'preciate ya helpin' here, Will. I was a gonner for sure."

Overwhelmed by what just happened, I blurted out, "He killed the first Chickadee, right over there. His body is lying in the snow by that log! That's where I got the knife. It was the knife that boy used for chipping. It was just like he was staring right at it so I would see it."

Frank walked with me over to the site and together we worked in silence for several minutes to uncover the decomposed remains of Chester.

When we finished, Frank said, "We'd better get to camp and call the sheriff out here. I been followin' Nyka on and off for a couple a days. He was lootin' the still. I knew it was some logger but didn't know who 'til now. The tracks he left was kinda odd. The front of one track had a vee shape like the bottom was split. I was headin' up to yer camp hopin' to check the boots of the boys, all discrete like. Then I sees these fresh tracks and though they was different, they still left kinda the same mark on the same boot."

Examining Nyka's boot, Mattson said, "Looks like he tried to fix 'em. Ya know that pea shooter of mine sure works a hell of a lot better on hares than it did on that cuss. Caliber's just too small ta bring down a big ol' boy like Nyka. I can't believe you kilt that son-of-a-bitch."

The months of chopping branches after my circuit around the trails each morning didn't make me a logger, but it did increase my strength. I guess I was strong enough, even as a scrawny eight-year-old, to drive that rusty knife through his coat and deep into Nyka's back.

22

Frank and I made it back to camp. We stopped at the kitchen first to have Mattie look at Frank's jaw, which was swollen and turning purple.

"Wha' happin' to you, Mr. Mattson?" she asked. "Ya get yourself kicked by a horse?"

"Nope. Nyka."

"That man is gonna kill somebody b'for too long," she said, shaking her head.

"No he ain't," Frank said. "Will here saw to that. He kilt 'em."

"You kilt Nyka?!" Mattie shouted.

"Yup. He took me to where he killed the last Chickadee, and I figure he was going to do the same to me."

Mattie left tending Frank. She reached out and pulled me into her bosom so tightly that any protest or attempt to escape would have been futile.

"Tha' son-of-a-bitch. Good riddance!" she said. "Are ya okay, Will? Did he hurt ya?"

I was able to answer only after she released me from her embrace. "No ma'am, but he was planning to."

Outside the kitchen hung a bell that was used to call in the crew and to help guide anyone who got lost in the swamp. Mattie went outside and rang it vigorously for several seconds. The men began emerging from the bunkhouse. John Bundy came from the office. Abraham ran the short distance from the barn and arrived first.

When most of the men were assembled outside the kitchen, Mattie said, "Nyka kilt little Chester and was goin' ta do the same ta Will here, but Will kilt him first."

"You killed Nyka?" Michael said, and walked over to me.

"I had to!"

Michael put his arm around my shoulders. "Did he hurt you?"

"Nope, but he wolloped Mr. Mattson a good one."

John Bundy and Michael simultaneously asked where it happened.

"About a quarter of a mile west of the road where it turns along the river," I said.

Questions were being shouted all at once. Michael stepped away from me, waved his arms and said, "Hold up for a minute. Let him just tell us what happened, we all want to know."

The group fell silent and every eye turned to me and Frank.

"Will, you tell 'em what happened. My jaw is swellin' shut and I sorta got there late anyway," Frank said, talking through his teeth.

After I had finished recounting what had happened, John Bundy said, "I better drive into town to get the sheriff. Will, you show the boys where Nyka is. Maybe he's still alive. We may need to get him to a hospital."

"Oh, he's good an' dead," Frank said.

"Well, we should be sure."

I started back down the familiar trail. This time, like a majorette leading a makeshift parade, I retraced the route I had just taken with Nyka. On the way I heard Mattie tell Abraham that that was the first time she had ever been out on the trail. As we marched, some of the men came up alongside of me and asked more questions about what had happened. Sven said he would believe Nyka was dead only when he saw Nyka's body for himself.

I was embarrassed by the unaccustomed attention, but felt so relieved to be out of that horrible situation. It was all I could do to not shout out loud in joy. Despite the adrenaline and blur of events, I tried to stay calm.

A short time after we returned to the scene, the sheriff arrived with two deputies in a truck. They managed to drive all the way down the trail to the point where they could see the crowd of us off in the woods.

The sheriff questioned Frank and me about what happened. I made it a point to tell the sheriff about seeing Nyka at seven-thirty the night the girl was assaulted at Margie's. The sheriff told us that initially the girl was so groggy from being knocked unconscious that her description of her assailant was too vague to be helpful. As her mind cleared over the next couple of days she was able to give a full description. It was Nyka to a tee. My information helped corroborate the timeline and further implicate Nyka.

When he finished his questioning the sheriff said, "There is only one law we enforce at whorehouses and that's don't hurt the girls. Margie don't call me every time a girl gets slapped around a little. That happens all the time. But if they're hurt and out of commission, that costs Margie a lot a money and that's when she calls in the law." Then the sheriff whispered to Frank, "I'm gonna need an extra bottle of *potato water* this week." Frank nodded.

The sheriff's crew exhumed Chester's body from the snow and put it in the back of the truck next to Nyka.

Finishing his work, the sheriff came and asked me if I was going to be okay. Still shaking, but recovering from the ordeal, I nodded my head. The sheriff smiled and said, "When you get a little older we just may have to get you on the police force. You already know how to deal with perverts and murderers."

Deiter caught up with me on the way back to camp and asked me jokingly, "Where was all that knife wieldin' skill when I coulda used some help back at the boarding house in New York?"

I made us both laugh when I uncharacteristically shot back, "I figured you could handle that by yourself."

126

Of all the comments from all the men, however, the highest praise came from Sven, who had said very little up until then. He patted my shoulder with that huge callused hand and said, "There's grow'd men that wouldn'ta been able to do what you did, son."

I remembered that comment whenever anyone called me Chickadee after that, or I started to feel sorry for myself. I drew encouragement from Sven's comment because maybe I wasn't so weak and helpless, maybe I could be a logger after all.

Talkin' about Nyka at lunch. *(Image BK058 from the collection of the German Settlement History Inc., Ogema, WI)*

Over the next several days the camp gradually returned to its routine, and references to Nyka faded from the major topic of discussion to an occasional comment, except for Abraham. He could not get enough information, and never tired of hearing the story.

It stayed light longer as winter sputtered to an end. I spent more time in the barn. Abraham and I would talk for hours about our dreams, fears, almost anything. Abraham's biggest fear was of losing his mother. I guess that would have been my fear, too, if I hadn't already lost mine. We had other things in common, too, like our love of horses. He wanted to be a teamster like Max, and added that he liked being around horses more than people, except for me and Mattie.

For me, I wanted to be a logger, to own and run my own lumber company. Running a logging camp was not a job for the weak or the faint of heart. Maybe I was becoming capable of making my wish come true.

23

During the first week of April, a minor jam of pine logs and ice upstream had gotten progressively worse. A week-long thaw raised the river level. The rising water broke up the ice and dislodged the logs that collected in the slow-moving sections of the river. The ice slabs and logs formed a dam where the river narrowed. The water backed up behind the tangled mess and flooded low areas, including the region Jason had scheduled next for cutting.

I was sharpening Nyka's old axe in the bunkhouse. The men gave it to me along with some of Nyka's other belongings. I think they gave me the axe so I would stop borrowing one every time I set out to trim branches. The axe probably didn't need sharpening, but I felt more grown up sharpening my own axe in a bunkhouse of loggers. Since I killed Nyka, I no longer had to be specifically invited into the bunkhouse in order to be there.

The men talked about the logjam. Some of the old timers said that jams used to be common when most of the harvested timber was pine. Every spring jams would occur. In the early days of logging, all logs were floated to the mill using the rivers. There were fewer rail lines then. The rivers were a convenient and free source of transport. Before Seely bought the Thunder Logging Company, the crew had cut a half section of second-growth pine and hemlock, which were piled near the river ready to be floated to Eau Claire whenever the jam was cleared.

Ready to float to Eau Claire. *(Image 969 from the collection of the German Settlement History Inc., Ogema, WI)*

Jason barged into the bunkhouse. He looked mad.

When Michael saw him, he said, "Say Jason, I've had the assessment on that Chippewa Section done for a while. We can go over it anytime you'd like."

"Don't bother me with that crap now. I've got bigger problems."

Jason walked past Michael over to John Bundy.

"John, why the hell is everybody sittin' on their asses? We've got a lot to do before the ground gets too soft to get the logs out."

"The floodwaters behind the dam is blockin' the north end of the trail. The men can't get to any of the lowland we were cuttin'. I sent Max to get dynamite from one of the iron mines. Should be back the day after tomorrow," John said.

"I have no intention of having everyone sittin' around waiting for Max to return from a hundred fifty mile round trip. Any of you boys had any experience breakin' up log-jams?" Jason said.

No one responded, until Tom Nelson spoke up. "Every logger here knows that jams are dangerous as hell. The force of the river and all the weight of them logs and ice create a terrible tension on the front logs of the dam. When you bust up the tension them logs'll surge and flip around like matchsticks. Dynamitin' is the only way to go."

Logjam. *(Spirit River from the collection of the German Settlement History Inc., Ogema, WI)*

"Don't tell me I hired a bunch of chickenshits. Well, I'll pay any man with the balls to break up that dam fifty bucks straight up," Jason said.

"I'll do it." Someone shouted from the back of the bunkhouse.

Deiter stepped forward. When he walked past, Michael said to him, "Don't do it. That's suicide." Deiter ignored his brother and walked up to Jason.

"When you want this done?"

"Well, right now would be jus' fine."

Several of us followed Deiter out of the bunkhouse and to the shed. He grabbed a five-foot pole with a clasp-cant hook, the tool of choice for moving logs.

"This ought'a do the trick. It'll move the logs, and I can use it to anchor me," Deiter said.

Michael offered to help his brother, but not before I heard him say, "You know how stupid this is? Jams kill a lot of loggers, Deiter. Don't do it!"

"Come on Michael, with your help this will be a snap."

"It'll be a snap all right. Your legs'll snap, then your neck. I'll do whatever I can to help, but I know a lot more about estimating board feet than how to break up logjams."

Everyone in camp went down to the river to look on, except Mattie. She claimed she had dinner to cook, but I think she just couldn't bear to watch.

I'd seen Deiter in action at the boardinghouse and I knew he was nimble, athletic, and fearless. He also had Michael. When we got to the river, the sound of water rushing over and around the jam, and the cracking and thumping of the logs made it difficult to hear anything. Michael warned Deiter again and then showed him a few improvised hand signals to use in case they could not hear each other over the din. Before Deiter tackled the jam, Michael sought out Tom. He had been logging for thirty years and had seen it all. He was glad to help.

"You boys done chit-chattin'?" bellowed Jason. "Let's get goin'. It'll take two days for the water to drain from the trails as it is. Let's go, let's go!" he said, more imploring than ordering.

Michael, Deiter, and Tom walked to the water's edge. I followed. Each man studied the complex physiology of the logjam. Deiter said he was looking for the best route to take while traversing the dam, while Tom and Michael discussed where the key log in the jam was. Each pointed to a different log they thought was primary.

They decided the best approach was for Deiter to first try to move the log Michael thought was key. It was the easier of

Which one's the key log. *(Photo provided by Mike Monte, Crandon, WI, private collection)*

the two options to get to and probably could be moved more safely. They shared their plan with Deiter, carefully pointing out the log they decided should be moved first. They gave Deiter a chance to rebut. He chose not to second-guess his brother and Tom.

Before Deiter set out onto the dam, Tom warned him that there was no way to know what the log would do once it was free of the force holding it in place. If this was the right log, Tom said, it would take just a few seconds for the bulk of the dam to give way. Once the logs were put in motion and gained momentum, there would be no way to escape.

Deiter nodded. He stepped out onto the dam, took deliberate steps, and used the hook on the pole to steady himself while he slowly moved from one log to the next. He ducked under a log protruding from the dam and arrived at the target log. He pointed to it and looked back to Tom and Michael for confirmation. They both nodded. About half of the log was sticking out through the dam at a thirty-degree angle. Tom motioned with his hands that Deiter needed to twist it free.

"If that's the log, Michael, he's gonna have to get back to shore quick, real quick," Tom said.

After stabilizing his stance, Deiter began to work. First, he tried placing the hook on the top of the log using his weight to push down. He hung suspended for an instant while he tried to wrench the log free. The log didn't budge.

Next, he put the hook on the log from underneath. This position enabled him to hold the pole, lift with his legs, and apply greater force. I could see the log slowly twist under his pull. He removed the hook to reposition it when the log shot out of the dam as though someone spit out a paper straw. The log Deiter was standing on lurched, nearly sending him into the river. Then no other movement. The noise of the river probably prevented Deiter from hearing the gasps and shouts from us standing on the riverbank when we saw the log dislodge and Deiter stumble.

Deiter stood in a ready position just in case he had to start his escape if the breakup began. He stayed frozen that way for several seconds waiting to see if there would be a delayed reaction. None came.

Deiter turned around and looked at Michael and Tom. Michael shrugged his shoulders. Deiter furrowed his forehead and shook his head, good-naturedly mocking his brother's log selection.

Deiter appeared unclear as to which log he should try next. He watched as Tom signaled that it was about two-thirds of the way across the dam. Deiter slid, climbed, and hopped his way to the vicinity of the log and then watched Tom for further instructions. Once Deiter reached the log, Tom directed him to move to the other side of it and to pull up as he did on the last log. Deiter positioned himself as directed and gave the target log a tap and watched for Tom's nod.

Deiter placed the hook under the log. Steadying his feet

and getting a firm grip on the pole, he lifted. The log lurched but just an inch or two and barely enough to be seen from shore. The log's sudden movement seemed to startle Deiter. He gestured back to Tom and Michael that the log moved, holding up his thumb and forefinger in approximation of the distance it moved. Tom gave him a thumbs-up and nodded, telling Michael that he was pretty sure that was the key log.

Deiter took a deep breath, steadied his feet, and gave another pull on the log. It lurched again, this time dislodging. The movement released some of the logs behind it, causing a tremendous downward force on the opposite end of the log Deiter was standing on. The end under Deiter's feet shot straight up and sent Deiter airborne. Simultaneously, the center of the dam collapsed and surged forward. Those of us on shore could only watch as Deiter's body soared above the river, which now churned, tumbled, and roared in a heaving turmoil of logs, ice, and water. Deiter disappeared from our view, obscured by the limbs of the giant hemlock trees that lined both shores.

Jason cheered at the success of the endeavor. Michael ran up the riverbank to see if he could catch a glimpse of Deiter. Scanning the water and seeing nothing, he ran down the river to watch for any sign of Deiter among the logs and debris that bobbed and boiled past him. In a short time he returned to Tom and where the dam had been. He had the look of a man who had just lost his brother.

Being shorter than the rest of the on-lookers, my view looking up was less impaired by the overhanging hemlock branches. I saw Deiter for an instant longer than they could.

I yelled to Tom and Michael, "I never saw Deiter fall back below the branches!"

Michael walked over to me at a spot on the bank with less overhanging canopy. He seemed stunned and without hope, but scanned the base of the trees on the opposite side of the river from where I had pointed. He saw nothing. But I thought he was looking too low and not in the trees. The last I had seen of Deiter he was much higher and I didn't see him fall back down.

I searched high in the branches of the trees on the opposite side of the river, where I thought his trajectory might have taken him. There, I saw something.

"See it! See it!" I shouted. "It's blue! See it?"

Deiter wore a navy blue coat, which was indistinguishable in the dark shadows, but his blue workpants, faded from washing and wear, were visible. Michael got behind me and looked along my arm as though it were a gun barrel he was sighting. He nearly knocked me down with an excited jump when he saw the spot of blue tucked in among the branches at least thirty feet over the river.

"There shouldn't be anything blue up in those trees except Deiter," I said. "How are we gonna get him down?"

Tom joined Michael and me. I reminded them that there was a small boat in the barn. Tom dismissed that idea. "The river's impassible, and it'll take a day or two for the reservoir to drain. We're gonna have to drive all the way around."

While Deiter was only one hundred and twenty feet away, we would have to drive two and half miles over potted gravel roads, cross the bridge, and follow old logging roads along the other side of the river in order to reach him. I knew the route well, having accompanied the Mattsons a dozen times while trapping and tending their still. We raced for the truck!

We ran past Jason who had assembled the foreman and crew chiefs. He glared at Tom, Michael, and me as we ran to the company truck.

Tom drove, I sat in the center of the front seat with Michael on my right. The truck sped, alternately bouncing, sliding, and skidding out of camp onto the county trunk road toward the bridge. Tom knew the main roads but I was able to help navigate us through the maze of logging roads we needed to traverse to get to Deiter. It took us nearly fifteen minutes to reach the clearing directly across the river from where we started.

We walked up-stream and scanned the trees that hung

136

over the river, looking for any sign of Deiter. We found him enmeshed within the branches of a hemlock over thirty feet above the river. Tom ran back to the truck to rummage through logging gear in a box in the back of the bed. He returned carrying ankle spikes, an eight-foot leather strap, and a coil of rope.

Tom told Michael that he planned to use the rope to lower Deiter from the tree.

"It's been a good spell since I've done this. Hope I haven't forgot how," Tom said, as he positioned himself at the base of the tree.

He looped the leather strap under his butt and around the trunk of the tree, kicked the spike strapped to the inside of his left boot into the tree, and hoisted himself up by his left leg. Tom kicked the spike on his right boot into the other side of the tree trunk a bit higher than his left. Putting all his weight on the spikes, Tom leaned forward until his face was nearly touching the bark, arms spread wide, each hand holding the strap as though he was about to hug the tree. This created slack in the strap, which Tom tossed up the trunk two feet and sat back to tighten the strap. Sitting against the strap and leaning on his left leg he pulled the right spike out of the tree, replanted it a foot higher, and then did the same with the left spike. He rhythmically repeated the sequence of leaning forward, tossing the leather strap higher up the trunk, leaning back and stepping the spikes higher, until he reached the first branches about twenty-five feet up. Once there, he swung his leg over the first branch, removed the strap, and climbed the rest of the way to Deiter.

Tom shouted to Deiter but there was no response. Tom straddled the branch and worked his way out. Once he reached Deiter, Tom pulled the limp body into a seated position. Even from the ground, I could see the large gash on the left side of Deiter's head. Tom called down to us that it looked like Deiter was still alive but unconscious. Michael and I watched as Tom worked to maneuver Deiter's leg from the fork of a small branch. He tied the rope around Deiter's feet and chest in such a way that when he was lowered, he would be in a sitting position. Once the rope was secured around Deiter, Tom looped it once around a branch just above his head. He lifted Deiter off the branch he was sitting on. His lifeless body fell a short distance before the rope holding him jerked taut. Tom lowered him straight down toward the river. Once Deiter was about four feet above the water, Tom used his foot to push the rope and make it swing. Deiter's body alternately moved toward shore then back out over the river. On the third swing he was close enough for Michael and me to grab the rope and guide him to the ground.

24

Two days after Deiter was injured, Michael and I returned to the hospital to visit him. We were happy to see that he had regained consciousness and he was happy to see us. He complained of having a throbbing headache and blurred vision. His arm was in a sling, which he said was to immobilize his broken clavicle, and a heavy gauze bandage covered the gash on his head, which he proudly noted required thirty-two stitches to close.

Deiter said the doctor told him that until his vision returned to normal and the head wound closed and stopped draining, he would not be released.

"You know your doctor bill is going to be a hell of a lot more than the fifty bucks you earned from that harebrained act," Michael said.

A nurse walked into the room and matter of factly announced, "Time to change your bandage and check for infection, Deiter."

"Michael, Will, this here is my favorite nurse, Anna," Deiter said. Michael looked at the tall, green-eyed, serious young woman with an intensity and interest I hadn't seen him display with any other woman. Deiter noticed it as well and just shook his head. It was one of the rare moments I can remember seeing Michael unintentionally betray what he was thinking.

I looked from Michael to the nurse and couldn't believe what I was seeing. It was my mother's face and she was dressed in white. I often had nightmares of my mother dressed in white letting go of my hand and walking away. This was not a resemblance, but *my mother's face*. I stepped back from the bed and ran from the room, convinced this couldn't be real. I wanted to get as far away from there as I could. I made it to the end of the hallway before months of repressed, pent-up grief from my mother's death burst out.

I thought I was growing up. Deluded myself into thinking that sharpening Nyka's axe made me a man. But I was just a scared little boy still not able to deal with what had happened.

Michael found me in a corner of the hallway crying, crouched in a fetal position, my back to the wall. "What the hell is the matter with you, Will?"

I don't think I answered. Michael leaned against the wall next to me and slid down to my level. He put his arm around me, probably not knowing what else to do. As a defense mechanism, I had tried to repress the memories and trauma of my mother's death. The months of repressed memories and emotions erupted simultaneously when I looked at that nurse and saw her face. I cried and buried my face in my hands.

After a bit, I regained some composure. Michael asked me if I was ready to talk about what had traumatized me. I sniffled, wiped my nose and eyes on my sleeve, and without looking at Michael told him, "That nurse looks like my mother. Not a little, but exactly like my mother! Her name is even the same."

Michael tried to reassure me. "Will, I lost my mother and father, too. I know how hard it is." Then Michael suggested for my sake and probably his, "Would it help if you talked to the nurse?"

"I don't know. It's just really hard looking at someone that looks so much like my mother." I didn't tell Michael about my nightmares. I don't think I ever told anyone.

"Let's try to talk a little with the nurse, okay, Will?"

I nodded and we went in search of her. She had finished

in Deiter's room and moved onto the nurses' station when we caught up with her. "Miss," Michael said. When she turned around, her expression was that of a woman miffed that she was being interrupted from her work and indignant at so bold an intrusion from some logger she had just met. Michael must have sensed it, too. He grabbed me and pushed me in front of him.

"Miss, my friend lost his mother several months back and was amazed at your resemblance to her. Isn't that right, Will?"

"Yes, ma'am," I said. "You have my mother's name, too—Anna."

The nurse seemed to relax a bit, but was, well, unnerved by Michael. When he smiled at her, she quickly looked away and turned back to me.

"Well, I am flattered that you think I look like your mother. I'm sure it's just a coincidence that we share the same name. What is your last name?"

"Heinlein. We lived in Frankfort."

It was Anna who looked surprised, even shaken, now. "I have an Aunt Anna Heinlein that lives in Frankfort. What was her maiden name?"

"Schmidt," I answered.

Anna looked at me as though I just said something obscene.

Michael saw it, too. "What's the matter?"

"I'm Anna Schmidt," she said.

"Do you know Friedrick Schmidt?" I asked.

"My father is Friedrick."

Within a moment or two of exchanging fragments of family history, it was clear that I was talking to my cousin Anna.

Michael could not hide his delight when Anna agreed to have lunch with us after she finished her rounds. Michael and I went back to Deiter's room to wait. Deiter rolled his eyes when Michael told him of our date with Anna to learn more about my relatives, and said, "Yeah, right."

The brothers listened to me outline the few details I had

about my uncle Friedrick and his family. Deiter interjected additional information he recalled from things I had said on the trip from New York. All I really knew for sure was that Friedrick married an American woman. They had three or four children and lived in Chicago before moving away.

Anna returned carrying a charcoal-colored coat and red scarf, a sharp contrast to her stark white uniform, hat, stockings, and shoes. I was more comfortable looking at her when she was not in all white.

The three of us left an obviously disappointed Deiter and walked to a restaurant a block away. Anna made small talk while we walked and told us about the hospital. It was originally established for Civil War veterans and later used as a sanitarium for influenza and tuberculosis patients. The population growth of farmers, miners, merchants, and loggers created demand for medical care. Family doctors were simply unable to reliably keep up with the demand for services due to the distances and rigors of travel in the north woods. A few widely scattered and poorly equipped hospitals like hers were established once there were enough lumber barons and wealthy merchants demanding medical services.

At the restaurant, Anna and I exchanged more family information. The shock and trauma of seeing my mother's face dissipated. As we talked I was amazed that her eyes, mannerisms, smile, even her laugh, were my mother's. Michael seemed amazed, too, but for very different reasons. Through chess and card playing, Michael had become skillful at picking up the subtle cues of body language from his opponents. Despite her cold aloofness, Michael was intensely focused, probably trying to discern her interest in him. Did she turn away too quickly or had she tried too hard to show disinterest? Michael was studying her.

Anna directed her conversation to Michael for the first time, but only maintained eye contact briefly before looking away, perhaps taken aback by Michael's disconcerting penetrating stare.

"Would it be possible for you to bring Will to my house

to visit? My family would love to meet Will. Father may have some thoughts on Will's future."

Michael tried to appear matter of fact but his vigorous nod was excessive.

"Okay then. I will see you both on Sunday afternoon," Anna said.

I couldn't stop talking all the way back to the lumber camp about how unbelievable it was to run into my cousin. In just a few days I would meet my uncle. I was about to fulfill the promise I had made to my mother. Michael nodded occasionally as I went on, but I suspect he heard little of what I said. His mind was on Anna.

Neither Michael nor I could wait for Sunday afternoon. I was excited to meet family, Michael eager to see Anna again. When we arrived on Sunday the first to greet us was the family's mongrel, Woodrow. Anna's little sister tried to hold the dog back and said, "Oh, he's a very good dog with the family, but he is not too fond of strangers."

The dog broke loose, ran toward me, sniffed my crotch, then jumped up and tried to lick my face. His tail waged a welcome to a new member of the family. Michael reached down to pet the animal but pulled his hand back quickly when greeted by a snarl.

After introductions, hugs, and tea, the girls showed me pictures and we exchanged stories and family lore. I was treated like visiting royalty by the Schmidt family. Anna told us how she had shared the events of that day at the hospital with her family. Her father was deeply saddened by the news that his little sister was dead and provided more family history. At the end of the evening Friedrick proclaimed to his family that I should live with them. He had already invited the Heinlein's to come to America to join his family, and a logging camp was no place for an eight-year-old boy to grow up. If I wanted to stay with them I would be welcome.

Caught up in the moment and letting my guard down, I blurted out something to the affect of, "I'm so goddamn glad I found you!"

I remember the wide-eyed horror on the face of every Schmidt in the room. Anna's mother, a devout Lutheran, spoke quickly and sternly telling me, "No one ever uses the Lord's name in vain in this house. You leave your cussin' outside from now on!" I sheepishly looked down and nodded. I remember thinking that this would be precisely what my mother would have said if she ever heard me talk like that.

The awkward pause in the conversation passed, and while I had to often catch myself, I never made that blunder again. I later learned that, while outwardly miffed, each of the Schmidt girls was somewhat humored by the incongruity of this crude language coming from "such a sweet little boy."

Despite my cursing, Uncle Friedrick reiterated his invitation for me to live with his family. While delighted, I was also apprehensive and Anna's mother must have seen it.

"Will, why don't you take a little time to adjust to the idea and get to know us better before you decide. We're your family but we are still strangers."

Friedrick agreed, "You're welcome to move in any time. But perhaps doing so in a couple of weeks would be best," explaining that this would give the family time to prepare my room.

Friedrick invited Michael out to the porch where it was quieter and he could light up his pipe. As they walked out Friedrick said, "I don't recall hearing about your relationship with Will." I could hear Friedrick on the porch talking to Michael from the couch in the parlor where I sat with Anna's sisters. I couldn't hear Michael because his back was to me, but could tell he was talking when Friedrick would occasionally nod.

Friedrick walked to the end of the porch, rapped his pipe on the railing and said to Michael, "Tell me about yourself." He re-lit his pipe.

Michael moved closer to where Friedrick had positioned himself and was a few feet from the open door leading back into the parlor. I could hear both men now.

Michael briefly talked about his family but went into greater detail about his studies, his conscription into the Russian Army to play chess, and his immigration to America. Michael spoke freely. His thinly veiled abhorrence and sarcastic descriptions of the Russians and army life seemed to humor Friedrick. At times I thought Friedrick was impressed with Michael, but I heard him say with obvious disdain in his voice, "So you're a Polack and a Bolshevik?" He said it as though those were the two worst possible afflictions.

I hadn't given it a lot of thought prior to that night but Friedrick's comments reminded me of those I periodically heard before I left Germany. Many neighbors referred to Poles as Polacks, joking about them as weak, impoverished subsistence farmers with little education. In short, inferior to Germans. But I couldn't understand anyone thinking that Michael, of all people, was inferior. That wasn't logical.

Anna came out on the porch to ask her father a question. She crinkled her nose at the pipe smoke. "Papa, didn't your family live in Frankfort before coming here?"

"Yes, and not far from where the Heinlein's lived."

"Please excuse me for a moment," he said. "I need some tobacco." The way Anna glared at him, she must have known he had no intention of returning. It was up to her to be hospitable to Michael.

25

"Are you two going to join us for a glass of schnapps?" Anna's mother asked, poking her head through the door to the porch.

"Mother, it's Prohibition!"

"Oh, this is a special occasion. Michael would you like a glass?"

"I would, thank you," he said, motioning Anna toward the door ahead of him. When the pair entered the parlor, Anna's mother said, "I thought you were going to help me with the dishes, dear."

"Why I am," Anna replied. She looked at the Bavarian clock on the wall and seemed astonished and obviously embarrassed to discover that she had been talking with Michael on the porch for nearly an hour.

Michael and I stayed until well after dark. On the drive back to camp we talked about my moving in with the Schmidt family. Michael joked that he wasn't sure if two weeks would be enough time for me to pack up my gear and prepare to move. We both laughed, agreeing the probable time it would take to pack was closer to thirty seconds.

Michael confided that he had been keenly aware of Anna's father's cold reception but got mixed signals from Anna. Outwardly she seemed curt and as cold as her father, but on the porch ... well, he wasn't sure. He told me that Friedrick didn't care too much for Polacks and Bolsheviks. According to Friedrick they were the scourge of Europe.

"I think Anna likes you, Michael."

"I sure hope you're right, Will. But I'm not sure."

Michael and I shared information we each learned about the Schmidt's. Michael told me that while on the porch, Friedrick told him that when Prohibition was ratified in January of 1919, his business in Chicago collapsed, even though the actual law was not enacted for a year. Friedrick delivered grain and hops to the breweries. With the law ratified, his customers gradually just used up existing inventory without replenishing it. Friedrick said he moved the family north to use his wagon teams, trucks, and farm contacts to start a new venture—delivering food and supplies to rural stores and logging and mining camps.

Anna was nineteen and the oldest daughter. Although she was a nurse, her real objective was to become a doctor, but she was unsuccessful in her attempt to gain admittance to the Medical School in Madison. She was rejected three times. Anna complained that women had won the right to vote but still couldn't break into male-dominated fields, like medicine. Her younger sisters remained at home, went to school, and helped their father run the business.

Michael said he thought that Friedrick's business must be doing very well. The mines and logging camps were in constant need of food and supplies. In the brief time they spoke on the porch, Friedrick said that he needed to add more trucks, although he would keep two horse teams to make deliveries when the weather and road conditions were too much for the trucks. He also needed a horse team to extract the trucks when they were stuck in mud or a snowdrift. While it was frustrating, Friedrick thought that it was those challenges that helped limit competition and enable him to make a good profit.

"He doesn't think much of me, but I admire what Friedrick has accomplished," Michael said.

26

One evening in late April, some of the men lingered in the mess hall after dinner. I was putting away the last of the dishes and Abraham was in the barn. My ears perked up when I heard the conversation shift from small talk to what the men thought Jason's plan was for the company. Sven said in his ten years with the company he learned to admire and respect Jack Seely, but not Jason. Other Seely veterans agreed.

"That asshole isn't a logger. He just wants to buy and re-sell cut-over land," Max said. "What do you think, Tauno?"

"I heard he's usin' the back pay due us Thunder guys to buy land. He's gonna screw us fer sure."

"Do any of you think Jason has the balls to defy Jack?" Sven asked.

"I don't think he's doing it so much to defy the old man but because, despite his cockiness, he knows damn well he can't manage a loggin' camp. Sellin' land is easier, more his speed," Max said. "He's just a greedy son-of ..."

The conversation ended abruptly when Jason and John Bundy walked into the mess hall.

"I need to talk to Michael," Jason said. "Where the hell is he?"

"He ain't back from checkin' the damage in the swamp from the flood yet," Max said.

"Shit. I need that timber assessment. John, you find

him, and tomorrow morning bring him to my office. You tell that Polack he better be ready to give that report."

"Yes sir," John said.

I had just put the last of the pots and pans away in the back of the kitchen when Jason and John walked past me through the kitchen and out the back door. John said, "One of the draft horses was restless and hard to work with today. I need to check on it."

Since I was going to help out Abraham anyway, I followed them to the barn.

As I neared the barn door, they were still talking so I stopped to listen.

"John, that Thunder Logging crew is a pain in the ass. Deiter's hurt and people are leavin' all the time to check on him. They're insubordinate, and Michael thinks he is hot shit since he lucked out in that chess match. Tomorrow after I get Michael's report on the timber value in those railroad sections, I want you to fire the Thunder crew. *Every last one of 'em.*"

"Fire every last one of 'em." *(Image BK51 from the collection of the German Settlement History Inc., Ogema, WI)*

"I'll do it sometime before supper," John said. He sounded skeptical, but must have decided not to question Jason after getting that order.

"What do ya want to do about the back pay and the money we owe 'em on the timber they cut before you bought 'em out?"

"Screw 'em. We *adjusted* the inventory so as far as anybody is concerned we don't owe them much, and most of 'em are gone or sittin' on their asses every time I turn around. Screw 'em!"

"That's nearly two months pay is all I'm sayin'," John said.

"I don't give a damn! Fire 'em. I'm not paying that crew anything. I need that payroll money to buy some cut-over land to sell to the Croats. By using the Thunder crew's payroll, my dad won't see any money missing until we've turned a sweet profit reselling the land. Just do it, John!"

"Yes sir."

As Jason turned to walk out of the barn, I walked past him as though I was just coming over from the kitchen.

"Where you goin'?"

"I'm here to help Abraham finish up in the barn, Mr. Seely." Then I stepped past him into the barn.

John called out, "Where the hell are ya, Abraham?"

"I'm right here, sir," he said, as he stepped out of the stall. Surprised to see Abraham and me right in front of him, John growled, probably to impress Jason, "Did you hear what Mr. Seely and I were talkin' about, boys?'

"No sir, I was workin' yonder," Abraham said.

"What 'bout you, Chickadee?"

"No Mr. Bundy, I just walked over from the kitchen."

"Well, if you're lyin' and you tell anyone what you heard I'll throw you both outta here, after a good whoopin', you un'erstand that?"

"Yes sir," Abraham and I said in unison.

Jason continued on his way back toward the office.

"Well, Abraham, I came out here to ask ya if you seen

anythin' odd about Ben," motioning toward the big chestnut draft horse. "He was hard for Max to control all day."

"Lizzy's a leakin' and givin' off a powerful smell," Abraham said, pointing to the huge mare in the next stall.

"You think he might have lovin' on the brain, do ya Abraham?" John asked, laughing.

"Yes sir, I do."

"When you hitch 'em tomorrow, keep Lizzy in the barn. We'll jus' make the loads smaller for a couple of days. That should fix it," John said.

"Yes sir."

John left the barn and headed toward the office.

I helped Abraham take the load of manure out back and dump it on the pile near the garden to age for a few weeks before Mattie would have us spread it. When we finished, we walked in the kitchen through the back door, checked to see if anyone else was around, and told Mattie the news about the pending firings.

"I like them Thunder boys," Mattie said. "There ain't no call for cheatin' 'em outta their pay and throwin' 'em outta camp with no warnin'. I don' suppose there's anythin' they can do 'bout it, though."

I went to bed but couldn't sleep. I tossed and turned most of the night and hoped Michael would know what to do when I told him the next morning.

As the crew was heading to breakfast, I ran up to Michael and asked if I could talk to him in private. Even though I was just a Chickadee, everyone knew that Michael was helping me move in with the Schmidt's and no one thought anything of it.

"Jason's goin' to fire the Thunder crew today before supper," I whispered. "He's not goin' to pay us either. He's gonna do it after he gets your report on that railroad land."

"What makes you think so?" Michael asked.

"Abraham and I heard him tell John Bundy last night in the barn."

"Thanks Will, I appreciate knowing this."

"What are we goin' to do?"

"We'll figure something out. It'll be fine. Don't worry about that, Will."

Michael didn't seem as surprised as I thought he would be. He didn't even seem riled. Maybe he heard the men speculating on Jason's plans like I had. I felt better after talking to him. His quiet confidence was infectious.

Later that morning John Bundy told Michael that Jason was in his office and wanted Michael's report on the timber value of the railroad sections. I had already made my circuit around the trail and shadowed Michael as best I could.

I hoped Michael would use the news I gave him to develop a plan, another of his bold chess gambits. I couldn't tell what he was up to but his rapid pace conveyed his sense of urgency. He found Tom and pulled him aside. Michael removed and unfolded a piece of paper from his pocket. He showed it to Tom. After looking it over, Tom spoke and pointed to the paper; Michael put the paper against a post and made revisions. Tom nodded when Michael showed him what he added.

I knew he was up to something. As much as I admired Deiter's courage, when the pressure was on, I trusted Michael the most. Deiter attacked problems fearlessly, Michael solved them logically.

An hour later, Michael stepped inside the small cabin that served as the camp's administrative office and rapped on the open door. When he entered, I walked over and leaned against the outside of the building next to the door. I looked in from the side of the step and hoped no one would see me.

Michael was seated in front of Jason's desk.

"So do you have the timber assessments for those railroad sections you walked a while back for me?"

"I do."

"Well, what the hell have we got there?"

"The timber is made up of mostly second growth but two sections are first-growth hardwoods, a hodgepodge of species. Some areas have been burned over and are primarily covered in jack pine. The southeast quarter of section thirty-one was clear-cut years ago but has a marketable mix of hardwoods with birch and poplar dominant, but plenty of oak and maple. The river bottoms and lowland lakes are the typical mix of tamarack, hemlock, and cedar. Based on twenty-two dollars per thousand board feet, the average acre would yield about six hundred and fifty dollars in gross income."

"What about the big pines that are supposed to be in there?" Jason said.

"There are some nice pines but they're scattered and their value is included in the numbers I gave you."

"My old man was told there's a whole section of big pine in there. Most of the old farts talk about it as common knowledge. Are you tellin' me they're wrong? There has to be big pine in those sections."

While I didn't know it then, Michael was setting up Jason.

"You want to bet?" Michael said.

I knew he had burned Jason twice before with similar wagers on the chess match and the inventory so I assumed that Michael was pretty damn sure about what he just told Jason. Evidently so did Jason.

"Well, son-of-a-bitch," Jason said. "I'm not goin' to bet. I knew there was nothin' to those rumors. My old man was just lookin' for any justification to piss away more money on timber inventory that costs a fortune to log. He even had me pay the land agent for the Wisconsin Northern two hundred bucks to hold that land and wait for us to make an offer before he puts it on the open market. I'll have John wire him that we're not interested. Thanks Michael, now get back to work."

Michael walked out of the office past me and found Tom Nelson. The two talked at length until John Bundy interrupted.

"You boys jibber-jabberin' instead of workin' again?" Before either could respond John said, "Go get yer Thunder

Loggin' crew together in the mess hall for a short meetin'."
As John walked away, I saw Michael wink at Tom.

Once the entire Thunder crew was assembled, John was quick to the point.

"Jason and I ain't been happy with the way things have been workin' out. Some a you boys work pretty good but most ain't worth a damn. We're firin' the whole lot of ya, startin' right now. You clear out yer stuff. I don't want anythin' funny. You be damn sure to leave anythin' that belongs to Seely. Me and my partner here," holding up a double-barrel shotgun that he'd stowed on the chair behind him, "'spect no trouble. There ain't gonna be no back pay neither. You didn't cut much timber when you was with Thunder and you didn't cut much for me. Now clear out!"

Even though I knew it was coming, I was still a little stunned. It didn't occur to me that we'd immediately be led out at gunpoint. As we walked out, Michael put his arm around me, "I heard a rumor that you might be quitting this dump and looking for a real job. Is that right?"

I was emboldened again by his confidence. "That is a fact. I am open to offers."

"Let's get packed up and get out of here then," Michael said.

Michael and I climbed into the front seat of Tom Nelson's old truck with our scant belongings in the back. That's when I learned about Michael's plan, which was hatched just hours earlier.

"Tom, do you think we can swing it?" Michael asked.

"I don't know. That's a lot of money. I've got twelve hundred dollars from my stake in Thunder, but I'm goin' to need a chunk of it just to keep things goin'. How much do you figure we'll need?"

"I think around thirty-eight hundred for the section and probably another thousand to start logging. I've got fourteen hundred in the bank in Hayward and Deiter has about two hundred and fifty. We'll need to stop by and let him know he's an investor."

Confused by the conversation, I asked Michael what they were talking about.

"We're starting a new logging company as soon as we can raise the money to buy a couple sections of land from the railroad. The railroad doesn't know just what they have and I forgot to tell Jason that there are over four hundred acres of virgin pine tucked back in there. Since Jason isn't interested, Tom and I are going to buy it. The railroad is selling it dirt cheap."

"I've got some money, too," I said with some pride.

"Oh. How much can you invest, sir?" Michael said.

"I've got four hundred and eighty-three dollars." Although I thought that was a goodly amount, I was worried it might seem like a pittance to Michael.

"What! Where would a Chickadee get almost five hundred dollars?"

"A bunch of ways. I still have some money left from my mother. I got paid for bein' a Chickadee sometimes when John felt like it, and I got seventy-five dollars that Nyka had on him that the men decided I should get, Nyka not havin' any family. I got money from Mattie for hares I brought in from trapping with the Mattsons, and ..." I stopped, reluctant to share my clandestine source.

"Yes? And?" Michael asked.

"And I found about eighty-five dollars of loose change on the floor in the outhouse, mostly Sunday mornings." Tom and Michael laughed.

"You are one enterprising Chickadee, you know that, Will?" Michael said. "We are still going to need another thousand at least to buy the land and more to start logging."

"I wonder if Frank Mattson would be interested?" I said, thinking out loud.

"I bet he has some moonshine money stashed away," Tom said.

"He does. While we were out trappin' he said that he didn't want to keep the money at his house. If the dry agents came by they'd confiscate it for sure. He believes they'd do the same if he had a bank account in town. So he keeps a stash of his moonshine profits hidden in the woods. He says there's enough to keep his missus and kids goin' if he has to go to jail."

"It's worth a try if you are comfortable raising the issue with him," Michael said.

"I don't mind. We're goin' to drive right by his place, why not stop in and ask him now?"

"Well, why not?" Michael said.

When our truck pulled off the road and went up the drive toward the house, Frank appeared from behind his shed. I opened the door and got out. Frank put down his rifle and walked over smiling.

"Hey there, Will. Who ya got there with ya?"

Just then the door to their shack swung open and Al stepped out. He held his hand up toward the sun to block the glare, and when he saw it was me, he waved. I waved back.

"You know Michael and Tom don't you, Mr. Mattson?"

"I surely do." He stepped forward and shook hands with each man.

I jumped right into the issue, not knowing how else to do it.

"We just got fired."

"Sorry ta hear that, boys."

"Don't be sorry for us. We're going to start our own logging business," I said, with the slightly absurd air of a proud businessman announcing a business expansion.

Frank looked at Tom and Michael for confirmation.

"That's right," Tom said. "Michael here did timber appraisin' for Thunder and Seely. Found a piece of railroad land that's bein' sold for a price that ain't in line with the timber on it. Ain't that right, Michael?"

"He's right, Frank. It's up near the Chippewa. Best timber I've ever seen. But we need at least one more investor and Will, well all of us, thought you might be interested in considering investing."

"You boys are catchin' me outta the blue. I've got a little money but I really need ta think this over. I ain't much of an investor."

"We understand," Michael said. "We'll be staying at Tom's tonight and heading up to Hurley tomorrow or the next day. If you decide this is something you'd consider doing, stop over tomorrow. We can discuss the details then."

"We appreciate you considerin' this," Tom said.

"By the way, how much you boys think ya need?"

"At least a thousand more for the land, then another thousand to begin operations," Michael said.

Frank nodded, "That's a lot a money, boys."

"Yes, it is," Tom said.

The men shook hands again and we got back into the truck. When I turned to wave at Al, I noticed that all eight of Frank's daughters were on the porch, lined up from tallest to smallest as if choreographed for our benefit. I didn't know it then but I would eventually marry the second little girl from the right, Sarah Mattson. She was the prettiest girl in Sawyer County.

We backed up, turned around and drove off. Looking at the brood, Michael shook his head. "Frank will never do this."

"You wanna bet?" I said.

"What? You think that meeting went well?" Tom asked.

"Sort of. If Frank had no interest in this, he would have just said so. He wouldn't have asked how much money we were looking for. He is definitely going to at least think it over."

"That is still a bet I would take. What are we wagering, Mr. Gambler?" Michael laughed.

"I don't have anything to bet beside the money and I want that for the business. How about if you win I'll do something special you ask me to do, and you'll do the same for me if I win?"

"Well, if it's reasonable. You, sir, have yourself a wager," Michael said.

When we arrived at Tom's place, Michael and I followed him up the front steps. He was greeted first by his dog that seemed so happy to see him that he would wag his tail right off. Tom's wife, Beth, on the other hand, was obviously surprised and a little miffed at having unexpected guests. Beth didn't seem to mind having people over but acted as though she was selfconscious about her appearance. She probably would have liked to have had a chance to run a brush through her hair, and maybe put on a nicer dress.

Tom introduced Michael and me as Beth fidgeted with her hair. After we all sat down at the kitchen table, Tom told her about being fired and of the plan to start the logging operation. She didn't look happy. Why would she be? Tom just lost his job and she showed little enthusiasm for the uncertainty of the new venture. After she made dinner for us, she sat in a rocking chair in the corner of the room and knitted. An hour later she went to bed. The men stayed up for several hours discussing the plans. I was nodding off so Tom led me to the back bedroom. It must have been after midnight when the men retired.

The next morning, finishing the last of the breakfast Beth made, we heard Tom's mutt barking out front and Tom got up to investigate. "It's Mattson," he said.

I was out the door running down the steps of the porch before Michael could get up from the kitchen chair.

"Hey Mr. Mattson. Hi Al."

Tom and Michael joined me and exchanged greetings with the Mattsons. After handshakes, Frank said, "I thought 'bout what you boys said yesterday, 'bout that timber land. That jus' might be somthin' I can help ya with. My north still was all busted up two days ago by dry agents. They's around and they think I been makin' liquor. I can't spend this money on another still and can't be buyin' taters, corn, and stuff, or they know for sure I been moonshinin'. So I'd jus' have ta leave that money buried doin' nuthin and me doin' nuthin' but trappin'. I been keepin' this money for my family if I git throwed in jail. But I reckin' there's enough to invest with you boys, too. Maybe with da free time I got thanks to the dry agents, I might be able to do a little work, too. Sorta like buyin' myself a respectable job. Who else would hire an ol' broken-down moonshiner anyway?"

Frank took a canvas pouch out of his pocket, pulled apart the twine holding the top of the pouch closed, reached in and pulled out a roll of bills held with a rubber band. He handed it to Tom. "That's 'bout two thousand dollars there," he said. "That's what you boys needed, ain't that right?"

"Frank, that is exactly what we need," Michael said. Then he glanced at me and saw what must have been a smug look. He smiled and raised an eyebrow at me, then leaned in and shook Frank's hand again. Tom looked stunned.

"Thank you, Frank. We can head up to Hurley right now to try to buy that land. If we get it, we should all walk the property. Can you come along with us?"

"I'd really like to." Looking at Al, Frank said to him, "You gotta check that trap line the next couple o' days, you un'nerstan?" Al nodded.

"Good, you'll want to sign the deed with us as a partner in the property and get a good look at the land. We'll be back to pick you up at your place in an hour. We're going to swing by the hospital first," Michael said.

27

Deiter was happy to see us and eager to have company. "You've got to get me back to the bunkhouse. I can't stand this layin' around here doin' nothin' day after day. At least there I can talk with the crew and poke around a little."

"Tom, do you think Deiter could stay at your place when we get back? Rehabilitate there for a week or so?" Michael said.

"Sure. I just need to let the missus know before we show up."

"Tom, why your place?" Deiter said.

Before Tom could answer, I said, "We got ourselves fired yesterday. The whole crew from Thunder. You're fired, too."

"Well, am I supposed to thank you?"

Michael laughed at my assessment of the events then gave Deiter more details.

"Jason's investing in land sales and isn't interested in logging. He won't need the full crew unless he buys more standing timber. He isn't interested in logging unless there is a windfall in it for him. Do you remember those sections I told you Sam Slaby sent me to check out just before you and Will arrived?"

Deiter nodded.

"We're buying just under two square miles with more board feet of timber than there would be on thirty square miles of typical forest. There's probably sixty-five to seventy million board feet at twenty-two dollars per thousand.

That's over two-and-a-half million dollars! Tom and I figure it will take an eighteen- to twenty-man crew to log four or five million board feet in a year. That's fourteen or fifteen years of work."

Why didn't Jason and his old man buy it then?" Deiter asked.

"Once I knew Jason was going to cheat our guys and Mrs. Slaby, well I just kind of forgot about the big pine when I gave him my assessment. If we get the land we'll hire as many of the Thunder crew as we can. Maybe some of the Seely guys will be interested, too. Sven said he'd quit in a heartbeat if we get the land. It'll be like Jason paying the crew their back pay only he won't know he's doing it. Yeah, I cheated him a little, but damn he earned it! This is poetic justice."

"You don't need to justify it to me," Tom said. "That son-of-a-bitch cheats everybody he can—the Slaby's, the crew, Croats, even his father. Screw him. What do you figure it'll cost to get that timber out?"

"Tom, I think the crew, rail transport, mill costs, and equipment will cost maybe eighty thousand a year for all expenses. Tops. We can make some pretty good money on this. Deiter, we're leaving this afternoon to see if we can buy the land. Are you in?" Michael said.

"Do I have a choice?"

"Nope."

28

After picking up Frank, we drove the hour and a half to the Hurley office of Wisconsin Northern, adjacent to the train depot and storage yard. My new business partners and I walked up the stairs to the office and stood by an empty counter for a couple of minutes before an attendant appeared. The young woman seemed surprised to see four people there.

"Can I help you?"

"You sure can. We're here to buy parts of a couple of the sections of land you have for sale near the Chippewa, section twenty-two and part of thirty-one and thirty-two," Michael said.

"You will need to speak with Mr. Labraski. Just one moment," she said. She walked to the back of the room and rapped quietly on the glass window of an office.

"Ned, there are some gentlemen here to inquire about purchasing a couple of sections of land. Should I send them in?"

There was a loud and brusque reply. "By all means, send them in."

Walking about halfway back she waved to us, "You can come back and see Mr. Labraski now."

There were two chairs in Labraski's office but I was the only one that sat down.

"So which parcel are you interested in?"

"Section twenty-two and adjacent parts of thirty-one and thirty-two near the Chippewa," Michael said.

Rummaging across the paper-strewn desk, Labraski found the document he was looking for. "Here we go. Let's see, Section twenty-two and parts of thirty-one and thirty-two. Looks like that parcel and a bunch more are already spoken for. We've got others available. You want a list?" he said, unaware of just how devastating his statement was to me, probably to Frank and Tom, too.

"Who are you holding the tract for?" Michael asked.

"Why, I can't tell you that, son."

"It's Seely isn't it?" Michael said.

Double-checking his list, Labraski looked back to Michael, saying, "What makes you say Seely Lumber and Land Company?"

"I left Jason Seely's office two days ago and he told me he had no interest in that land and in fact he said he was sending you a telegram confirming that."

"Miss Ashcroft, will you come in here please?" The young woman reappeared at the door.

"Did we get any telegrams that I haven't seen yet?" he asked.

"Yes, sir, three arrived just after I got in this morning. Would you like to see them?"

"I surely would."

She returned in a moment with the telegrams and handed them to Labraski. He scanned the first, smiled and put it aside. Then he glanced at the second. "Here it is." He read it to himself, and then said, "It's from Seely's foreman, Bundy. Says just what you said it would, young man. Well I s'pose that section is back on the market then. That's land I'm not familiar with personally. Have you seen it?"

"I have," Michael answered.

"Excellent. The railroad will need $3,880. That includes closing costs and transfer stamps. Prices are not negotiable. Now, how are you gentlemen planning on paying for that land?"

"I s'pose cash oughta work," Tom said.

Labraski leaned back in his chair and folded his hands

on his fat stomach. "Cash?" he said, looking at Tom as if for the first time. "Cash works best!" His shoulders shook with laughter. "Yup, cash always works best."

After half an hour of copying legal descriptions, securing stamps and signatures, and filling out forms, the four of us walked out of the railroad office with a deed, title for the property, and a receipt of payment. To avoid any problems, Michael insisted that we register the deed at the county courthouse immediately, and we did.

Tom suggested that after registering the deed and once we walked the property, we should stop by the old Thunder Logging Company attorney in Phillips to have him draw up a formal agreement. The men all agreed that was a good idea.

While driving to the land the men discussed the details and terms they would like to have in the agreement. They joked some and were in a buoyant mood, but they talked seriously about business matters and decided how they would divide up interest in the company. Michael would be the general partner with forty-five percent ownership. Tom and Frank would be limited partners, with twenty and twenty-five percent respectively. Deiter and I would be non-voting investors each with a five percent stake. They would name their company P.M. & N. Logging, for Pzybylski, Mattson and Nelson.

29

We drove as far as the old logging road would take us and parked the truck. Michael led us down an abandoned rail line another mile before we arrived at the southwest corner of the section adjacent to section twenty-two. This was the access point to the forest we had just bought. The rolling hills in front of us were covered in maple, birch, and poplar ranging from six to eighteen inches in diameter. There wasn't one of the one hundred and thirty foot pines Michael had promised in sight. The trees looked no different than most of the timberland we were all familiar with.

"Michael, this is some nice woods but it ain't nuthin' special," Frank said.

"This is the only way in. We're not even on the parcel yet. Once we're past the hardwoods we'll reach the pines. Don't worry."

But as we walked another quarter mile through the forest, I could tell the partners were beginning to worry. "Haven't we walked far enough yet?" I asked, voicing the collective concern of the others.

"Just about," Michael said.

Along the shoreline of a lake that abutted the west side of the property, we encountered a stand of conifers towering over the lake.

"Are those the pines?" I asked. "They're huge."

Tom picked a tick off his neck, crushed it between the fingernails of his forefinger and thumb and flicked it to the ground, and said, "Nope. Them's cedars."

We walked up the slope that led away from the lake and

saw the first pine trees. Some were a good size but most were ordinary and just mixed in among cedar and spruce.

We crested a hill and there it was. I looked in awe at a completely foreign forest. Instead of the raspberry briars, ferns, and brush we had been fighting through, we were on a forest floor of matted pine needles and except for a few fallen branches and enormous moss-covered logs, the forest floor was empty. The forest was silent except for the distinct tapping of a pileated woodpecker. Above us was a canopy so thick that it seemed like we went from mid-day to dusk in a few steps. The first branches of the canopy were fifty feet above us. The tree trunks were all three, four, as much as seven feet in diameter. Only Tom had ever seen any of the old growth that once covered the entire area just seventy years earlier.

Frank, who had expressed more than a little concern as we walked in, turned to Michael and broke the silence, "Holy shit, I ain't seen nuthin' like this, ever. I can't believe we own it! You sure weren't whistlin' outta your pant leg when you described this, Michael."

I was amazed at the size of the trees. Thinking back to the landscape I watched pass by on the long drive from the rail station to the logging camp, I said, "What a shame this will all be cut-over stumps and stubble one day."

"When we're all sittin' in our fine homes a sippin' champagne, none of us will give a shit," Frank answered laughing.

Evidently, Michael had given that subject some thought. He told us his professors in Krakow had developed some forest management techniques, mostly out of necessity since Europe's timberland had been exhausted through centuries of exploitation.

Looking at me but speaking to all of us, Michael said, "We don't have to take it all out. We can manage the logging so the smaller pines are left for the time being. Actually they'll grow a lot faster once the canopy from the tallest trees is broken, so there is no good reason to clear-cut. The growing trees can give us sixty thousand more board feet every year just by growing. If we do it right, we can log profitably way beyond fifteen years. Hell, our kids could be loggin' pine in here a long time from now."

We drove from the property to Phillips to get the partnership agreement drafted. Frank was giddy during the drive. By my count he thanked Tom and Michael five times. He even thanked me. Michael had seen the land twice before and Tom and I had learned from past experience to trust Michael's judgment. He was always reliable, pragmatic, and precise. Neither of us had much doubt concerning the accuracy of Michael's description and assessment of the land— but Frank was just learning that.

Old growth pine. *(Image 098000007-1 from the Wisconsin Historical Society)*

30

Two days and three hundred miles of driving later, Michael and I walked back into Deiter's hospital room eager to tell him the news, but he wasn't there.

We walked down the narrow hallway and found him sitting in a waiting area. "Hey gentlemen!" Deiter shouted as we walked toward him. "I am able to get around pretty well by myself, my vision is back, and the stitches aren't oozing anymore. Get me the hell outta here."

"That's why we're here," Michael said. We started to walk slowly back to Deiter's room.

I couldn't wait and blurted out the news, "We got the land. All recorded and legal like."

"Well, well, well. Sounds like we're in the loggin' business."

"Yup," I said. "Walked all over the land last week. Deiter, there are trees bigger around than your bed! Right Michael?"

"Its first-growth timber alright. We think that we should probably start with the front six forties that are mostly hardwoods. They're smaller, we won't need heavy equipment, and they're easier to get to. We can use the income from the hardwoods to buy a decent Caterpillar or Allis Chalmers rig to clear a road and eventually to help handle the pine. Doing it that way is a lot cheaper and we generate income with our first load of hardwood. We can pay ourselves and crew as we go."

Anna walked in. She visibly lit up when she saw Michael. Ever since her father had abandoned her on the porch with

Michael, her coolness toward him had subsided. With each successive visit to the Schmidt's house, she grew more relaxed around Michael. She was clearly quite fond of him. It was obvious that she missed him when he didn't come by during the past several days.

"Hi Anna," Michael said.

"Hello Will, hello Michael," Anna said. "How are you doing today, Deiter?"

"I'm climbin' the walls."

"Well you shouldn't be doing that in your condition," Anna said.

Michael laughed at her joke, more than what was warranted.

"Well I am. Michael's planning on taking me to a friend's house, hopefully today," Deiter said, looking at Michael.

"That's why we're here," Michael said.

"He can check out anytime now," Anna said. "Will, have you given some thought to my father's offer to come stay with us? We would love to have you."

"I'd be very pleased to stay with your family, Anna. My mother would be happy knowing that somehow I found you. We haven't been by to visit for a while because we were busy. Yup, we're starting our own logging company. Mostly because we all got fired from our jobs."

Anna shot Michael a look of disappointment, touched his arm and asked, "Michael, what happened?"

Michael sounded like he wanted to set the record straight. "We are working for another logging company now. We closed on a land purchase two days ago and will begin operations in a month or two. But the sooner the better."

"And it's our company, too!" I chimed in. "You should see the trees. They're as big around as this here bed! Hundreds of 'em. Right Michael?"

"Actually, about eighteen thousand," Michael said, trying to sound matter-of-fact. "We have five investors. The three of us, the old foreman from Thunder Logging, and a friend of Will's with some money to invest."

"Father is always looking for investment opportunities in new companies since the stock market has been such a bust," she said. "Why didn't you ask him?"

"Invest with a Polack Bolshevik? I don't think so," Michael said. He seemed to enjoy saying that a lot more than Anna liked hearing it.

"Actually we did think of your father, but we felt it was a little brazen to discuss investing since it had been such a short time that we've known you, and to be honest, your father doesn't like me much."

Anna didn't deny Michael's assessment, but said, "Well, you should have asked anyway."

Michael had met Anna's father a few times. Each time Friedrick was brusque, but he had grown outright hostile as Anna's attraction became more obvious. For that reason Michael much preferred meeting Anna for lunch or at the hospital where he didn't have to endure Freiderick's icy stares and derogatory sarcasm.

She looked for a second as though she was going to take Michael's hand, but she caught herself. "So where is this property? When will you begin logging? Where will you live?"

"Anna, I hope to be coming by with Will to move him in with your family. We can tell you all about it then." he said.

"Well, of course. Will can move in anytime he wishes."

"How about tonight?" I said.

"Tonight would be just fine, Will," Anna said. "Michael, can you bring him by tonight?"

"Sure can and we can talk about the business venture then."

"That would be fine. I need to finish my shift and let my parents know you're coming," Anna said.

Before she left Anna gave me a hug, and blushed when her eyes met Michael's.

31

Whenever they needed an extra pair of hands, Michael would pick me up at the Schmidt's and I would stay a night or two in the makeshift camp. I slept on the floor of the shed or in an army surplus tent Frank had traded for some pelts. The incessant buzzing and biting of the summer swarms of mosquitoes and deer flies, and wood ticks crawling up my legs, nearly drove me crazy. Frankly, I preferred to work in the woods in the bitter cold and snow than fight this losing battle with the bugs. The bugs didn't seem to bother the men as much, so I tried, with only limited success, to suffer in silence.

Michael's plan was working just as he had envisioned. The five of us and a small crew cut timber all summer and brought a load to the mill every two or three weeks. This generated income to pay the men and cover operating expenses, with enough extra to put money down on the purchase of some much-needed equipment. We cut the timber nearest the road first, slowly working our way toward the stand of pines.

After bringing me back to the Schmidt's from the camp Michael would visit Anna. The two spent considerable time together.

Uncle Friedrick appeared to be increasingly outraged that Anna had taken a liking to Michael. On one particularly hot afternoon in August, Friedrick saw Anna and Michael kissing on the porch. His self-restraint must have given out.

"With all the decent young men in this country, my daughter latches on to a dumb Polack," he said, loud enough to be heard throughout the house and porch.

Anna walked into the parlor and, nearly nose-to-nose with her father, shouted back, "The only dumb one here is *you*! Michael is ..."

Her father slapped her face before she finished. She fell across a coffee table breaking an ashtray and sending pieces of the glass, Friedrick's pipe, and ashes across the floor to where I was seated petting Woodrow.

Hearing what transpired, Michael ran into the room from the porch and pushed Friedrick in the chest. He fell awkwardly into a chair. Woodrow barked, and I grabbed his collar before he could intervene.

Anna's mother jumped between the two men and pushed Michael back toward the porch.

"This is a family matter and you best leave," she said.

Michael looked at Anna, who gave a barely discernable nod affirming her agreement with her mother's order. He turned and left.

Anna didn't cry. She was probably just as stubborn as her father. Her face showed a determination that indicated she had no intention of succumbing to her father's wishes or letting that episode pass unchallenged. Her mother must have seen it, too.

Gretchen was a strong German woman, but during the time I spent with the family she had always been deferential to her husband. She appeared content with her secondary role in a paternalistic household—except for then.

She stepped in front of Friedrick who was on his way out the door after Michael. "Friedrick Schmidt, you're a bigoted old fool. That man has done nothing to you and has been a perfect gentleman. But not you!"

"Get out of my way, so help me," Friedrick said through his teeth.

"Are you going to smack me, too? Because that's what you're going to have to do to make me move."

Friedrick hesitated, but evidently chose not to escalate the chaos he created. Gretchen's actions were so uncharacteristic it must have surprised him. While I was living there, he often went to her for counsel. When she offered an opinion to him or raised an issue, Friedrick responded in a way that made me think he viewed her input as level-headed, well considered, and of value. The fact that she chose that instance to defy him, probably for the first time in thirty years of marriage, gave him pause.

Based on the reaction of the family, I had just witnessed a watershed moment. Friedrick looked down at Anna, who had been joined by her two younger sisters, each hugging her in support. The trio glared at him defiantly, and his wife stood before him with steely determination.

After several seconds, he pushed aside the displaced chair he had briefly occupied, walked out the back door, slammed it, and headed in the direction of the barn.

I had heard Uncle Friedrick make disparaging remarks about non-Germans, but passed it off as an attempt to be funny or German pride. I had heard similar diatribes back in Germany, and from Jason and others. But he flagrantly insulted Michael and Deiter, the two men who took me in as family when I needed someone most, and to whom I owed everything. So he was insulting me, too. Despite his hospitality to me, I didn't like him then, and that never changed.

He went to church every Sunday and made me go, too, whenever I was there. He nodded to the scriptures when read, he insisted on the adherence to Christian ideals, but at the same time he hated my friends. Whether he was my uncle or not, to me Friedrick was just a hypocritical old man and depending on how this played out, I was prepared to move, too, maybe to the Mattson's.

Anna's assessment may have been similar to mine because it seemed clear to me at that moment that if being with Michael meant losing touch with her father, so be it. Her mind seemed made up.

32

That night, after a brief and icy silent dinner, everyone prepared for bed. My room was at the rear of the house off the summer kitchen and behind Friedrick's and Gretchen's bedroom. In the wall between the rooms was an air duct. The duct was connected to the tin work leading to the coal furnace in the basement. The duct in each room was covered with an ornate brass grill to allow the easy passage of air. It also had a flap that could be lowered or raised to regulate the warm airflow to the room. I learned that when the flaps of adjoining rooms were open, if I laid on the floor next to the one in my room, I could hear the conversation as though I were in the room.

There was a great deal of tension in the house and it concerned the most important people in my life. While welcomed into their home as family, I was excluded from most private conversations. I felt uncomfortable and wanted to learn what I could. That night I listened at the duct.

Gretchen broke the silence, "You know Friedrick, Michael reminds me a lot of you."

"That Polack?"

"Yes, that Polack," she said. "He is quite good looking you know, just like that tall handsome German boy I fell in love with. You are selling this young man short, Friedrick. He has a fine education, and he is very interesting to talk to if you would take the time. But the most important thing is that your daughter loves him. Anna's a woman, a good woman. She is not one to be smitten on a whim. She sees the substance in Michael."

"She knows how I feel about Polacks, but she persists anyway!"

"Friedrick, unfortunately your opinion on this matter is not relevant to Anna."

Friedrick muttered something, but I couldn't make out what he said.

"Don't put her in a position of having to choose between love and estrangement from her father. Just think about it," Gretchen said.

She must have blown out the kerosene light, because the sliver of light coming through the vent went out, and the conversation ended.

33

Anna had become pensive and withdrawn since her father's condemnation of Michael, but she still confided in her mother. While doing the dishes in the kitchen after baking, Anna and her mother talked about shopping and clothes, which I had little interest in, and didn't really listen until the topic changed to Michael.

They seemed oblivious to me sitting at the kitchen table quietly playing with Chester's old toy soldiers while eating a cookie.

Anna brightened up when she talked about Michael, which seemed to make her mother happier as well.

"Michael seems so serious, he's hard to read," her mother said.

Anna replied, "He was at first. It's like he's playing chess with the whole world. Afraid to reveal too much or the game would be lost. But he's really just shy and naïve, like a little boy in some ways, especially around women. Yet he is so smart, so perceptive in other ways."

"He didn't have any sisters, did he?" her mother asked.

"No, and living on a small farm, then going to a boys' school, didn't help either. But when we talk, he listens. He seems to know what I'm thinking. I start to explain something about how I feel, or a problem at the hospital, or even father, and he understands. Not condescending, he really understands. It's like he can see through me, through my eyes."

Her mother just nodded while Anna spoke.

After a moment of silence Anna's voice turned serious. "What if we just eloped?"

Her mother did not seem surprised by the question. After overhearing the conversation she had with Friedrick, I realized that she walked a fine line between loyalty to her husband, their traditional family values, and empathy for her daughter's dilemma.

"Don't do something you will regret for the rest of your life, dear," she said. "Get your father's blessing."

"He won't ever accept Michael!"

"Never say never, dear."

Her mother seemed to suggest there was at least some hope. Although she probably didn't know what Friedrick would do if he was asked to give his blessing, I think she felt her conversations with Friedrick were having some influence.

34

Since May, when I moved in with the Schmidts, other than a few chores around the barn, I was able to go to work at the camp anytime Michael would take me. That freedom ended in September when the Schmidts enrolled me in school, just before I turned nine. I was placed in the third grade. I spoke English fluently after a year, but I was not at all proficient in reading and writing, and was well behind the other kids. The Schmidt girls took turns tutoring me on my schoolwork every night. I tried to do well but struggled. Anna asked one evening how I liked school. I told her I didn't like it at all.

"Why don't you like school?"

"They're all just little kids," I said.

She laughed. I didn't think what I said was funny. I hated school and wanted to be with Michael and Deiter in the woods.

At least I could look forward to the weekends when Michael drove back from the site to see Anna, and would take me with him when he returned.

One Saturday afternoon at the end of September our old nemesis John Bundy came by our new logging operation. I saw him when he pulled in and greeted him, though not very politely. He asked if he could talk to Michael. I led him to the shed where Michael and Tom were talking. The shed was our office, mess hall, storage barn, and bunkhouse.

I sat on a tool-chest on the floor, curious about what

John had to say. He congratulated Michael and Tom and told them that Jack Seely had taken the loss of the land pretty hard.

"I feel real bad that Jason cheated you and your crew-mates outta your back pay. That was wrong. But you got him back good," John said.

Even before being fired, Tom made no secret of the fact that he couldn't stand Jason and had a low opinion of John Bundy for doing his bidding. Tom was not going to just let it go.

"John, you know damn well it weren't just the back pay. Jason cheated me, the crew, and Mrs. Slaby by havin' your crew mismarkin' Thunder timber at the mill and payin' less for the company than you knew it was worth. You an' Jason screwed us outta pay for timber we cut and then sayin' the crew wasn't worth a damn. You cheated Michael on that bet about the inventory, too."

"I ain't real proud of some of that stuff neither, and I understand what you're sayin' Tom, but I don't want there to be hard feelin's. This business ain't always pretty, and you know that all kinds of shit goes on," John said.

"I suppose we made Jason look pretty foolish," Michael said.

"That ain't the half of it," John said.

John told us that right after we bought the land he and Jason went to talk to Jack Seely. Jason walked through the house and out onto the back porch where Jack usually sat. John said he waited inside but heard everything.

"The first thing Jack says is, '*You did what? You stupid shit! How did I raise a kid that's so damn stupid?*' So Jason tells him that Michael looked over that section and gave him the report that said the land was nothing special, with just a few pine. So he had me wire the land agent figurin' there's no reason to burn that bridge. Then Jack says, '*You bring that son-of-a-bitch assessor in here, I want to talk with him!*' But Jason says he can't. Jack says, '*Why the hell not!*' Then Jason tells Jack he fired Michael and the entire Thunder crew. Jack says, 'You cost me a hundred thousand dollars, probably more, you dumb shit. How you gonna get that money back sellin' forties to Polacks? Jeezus Christ, I can't believe this. I paid that numb nuts railroad agent two hundred bucks to hold that property, and you go send him a wire tellin' him oh, just forget the whole thing.' Then Jack calls me out onto the porch. He tells me to hightail it up to Hurley and see if that property is still available. If it was, I was s'posed to tell 'em that Jack Seely wants it and guarantees whatever it takes to have the railroad hold the property till he personally gets there with a check. If it was sold, I was s'pose to see if that deed was registered yet. If it weren't, I was to find a way to queer the deal. Then Jack says to Jason, 'You better hope that land ain't been sold. I still own this company! I let you do some managin' while I was stammerin' and slobberin' on myself after that stroke. Even when I started gainin' back some feelin' in my face and arm I thought I'd leave ya' in charge. But you just want to fiddle fart around tryin' to sell horseshit land by callin' it Shangri-La. I was hopin' I'd be long dead before you was able to ruin the company. But you turned out to be a whole lot better at screwin' things up than I ever suspected. Congratulations, boy. Now get the hell outta here before I pop another blood vessel.' That's when Jason and I left."

By the end of John's story Michael and Tom were laughing, but I couldn't tell if it was John's imitation of Jack Seely or the ordeal Jason went through. I never met Jack Seely.

John told us that after checking with the county clerk and seeing there was little Jack could do, he returned to report back.

"I told Jack that you boys did everythin' you needed to do and that land was sold, closed, and recorded. He asked me who bought it and after I told Jack who it was he says, 'Pzybylski's the one who gave Jason the report, ain't he? I figured it was him or someone he was workin' for. I jus' didn't figure him for havin' the money to buy over a section. They either knew Jason was goin' ta fire 'em, or they were goin' ta quit

Passing through Shangri-La. *(Image BK073 from the collection of the German Settlement History Inc., Ogema, WI)*

as soon as they got the land. Either way, they outsmarted us. Shit!'"

John went on to say that Jack seemed to resign himself to what happened when Jack said, '*You know, I almost wish I hadn't lived to see just what a dumb shit my kid is. I hoped in a few years he might wise up a little. But that stroke didn't give me the chance to wait. His mother thinks I'm too hard on the moron. But Jeezus Christ ...*'

"Then Jack thanked me and I haven't seen him since. I hear he's gotten pretty sick."

After finishing his story, John congratulated Michael and Tom again. Wished us luck and said he needed to get going and repeated, "I hope there ain't no hard feelin's."

When he was gone, Michael asked Tom if he thought John was looking for a job or wanted to get a look at the operation.

"Both," Tom said.

35

Friedrick spent a lot more time in the barn than he had before he slapped Anna. Otherwise he acted as though nothing had happened. On the surface, the family was back to their routine with no outward sign of the tension that seethed just under the surface. Whenever Michael and Deiter came by, Friedrick found a reason to putter in the barn. Michael rarely came into the house. When he did, Anna would meet Michael on the porch or driveway, and they would take walks or he would drive them to town for lunch.

On a Saturday morning in the second week of October, Friedrick looked out the front window of the parlor while he relit his pipe. I sat on the floor of the parlor cleaning the mud off my boots and off the floor where I tracked it in— Gretchen's orders.

Friedrick saw Michael's truck pull into the drive, and as he had done many times before, turned to retreat to the barn. Before he reached the back door, we both heard running footsteps on the hardwood floor of the upstairs hallway. Friedrick turned to scold the culprit. Anna was running down the stairs, oblivious to our presence. The joy on her face as she ran to greet Michael made her look radiant, and the contrast with the hateful stare she had given her father a few weeks before was obvious to me and probably to Friedrick.

I thought I saw tears well in Friedrick's eyes. While he rarely showed his emotions, anyone could tell he adored his

Friedrick's Sanctuary. *(Image Duane033 from the collection of the German Settlement History Inc., Ogema, WI)*

girls. I don't think he could avoid the wonderful feeling a father gets when seeing one of his children so happy.

He left without a word.

A couple of hours after Anna had rushed out to meet Michael, she came back into the house alone. Gretchen asked me to go to the barn to let Friedrick know dinner would be ready in a few minutes. While running out to the barn I was distracted by some animal tracks in the mud. Frank Mattson had shown me tracks like that, perfectly round and an inch in diameter. He said they were from a red fox. I walked along the line of tracks next to the barn thinking where Frank might have chosen to put a trap. Then I noticed Michael walking by himself toward the front of the barn. Curious about why he would go to the barn, I lost interest in the fox and went into the open door on the side of the barn.

Friedrick was hunched over an old carburetor. That was the usual way he busied himself whenever Michael visited.

He looked up at the sound of one of the large double doors at the front of the barn sliding open. The bright sunlight silhouetted Michael.

"Mr. Schmidt," Michael said loud enough for me to hear.

"Yeah, I'm here."

Michael approached and put out his hand to shake Friedrick's. To my surprise, Friedrick put out his hand and shook Michael's.

From the back of the barn I could see the men's gestures as they spoke, but now that they were face to face and speaking normally, I couldn't hear their conversation.

Friedrick turned away from Michael and toward me. He looked amused. Maybe it was Michael's excessively long handshake or the fact that he tripped as he left the barn, or maybe he was proud of himself for calling him a Bolshevik Polack again.

"Dinner's ready in a few minutes, Mr. Schmidt!" I shouted.

He waved his hand to acknowledge my announcement. I ran back to the house to wash up for dinner. I waited for him to tell us what he and Michael had talked about, but he said nothing and I thought better of bringing it up.

36

Deiter and I sat in Woodrow's and my favorite spot on the floor in the Heinlein's parlor. It was where the sunlight came through the double windows on the south side of the house. We talked. I complained to Deiter about school and then remembered the bet I made with Michael that Frank Mattson would invest in the land purchase. Deiter had been in the hospital at the time so I told him all about it.

Michael and Anna returned from a walk on a sunny cool afternoon in the middle of October. After Deiter and I watched them share a long kiss on the porch, they turned to come inside. They probably hoped no one saw them. Deiter rolled his eyes at me and we continued to talk.

In the living room they found us deep in a discussion. I was surprised that Michael came in. Ever since Michael pushed Friedrick last summer, Michael rarely came into the Schmidt house.

Anna excused herself and Michael joined Deiter and me. "What have you two been discussing so intently?" he asked.

"We were about to ask you the same question," Deiter said.

"I'll tell you, Michael," I said. "You remember that bet we made on Mr. Mattson investing in the business?"

"I remember. It's a bet I regret. I should have known better than to take on a wily Chickadee," Michael said. "Have you decided what it is you want from me as payment?"

"Nope. That's my problem. I can't decide between two things."

"Well, what are the options?" Michael asked.

"I just can't decide if I want you to never call me Chicka-dee again or ... if you're going to have to marry Anna."

Michael laughed a long time, and then said, "Well, Mr. Wilhelm Heinlein, I believe sir, you will be getting two for the price of one wager."

With that simple exchange settling a bet, my year as a Chickadee ended. It sure didn't seem like a milestone then, but from that point on my life transformed from chaotic and unpredictable to traditional, although I was the only kid I knew in elementary school who worked weekends and summers as a logger.

Epilogue

I lived with the Schmidts until I was old enough to move out and buy a place closer to the land we owned. I finished school and married Sarah Mattson. We have two boys of our own, Mike and Peter. Michael and Anna built a beautiful Victorian home using lumber cut from our property. Sven did the finishing carpentry. What a craftsman! Michael's and Anna's home was bigger and grander than I think Anna was comfortable with. But Michael insisted. He calls it "Polack Manor." I think it was his way of snubbing his nose at Friedrick. They have three girls. Michael continues to run the business and Anna teaches nursing. Tom retired after he broke his hip and lives comfortably from the income he gets from his shares in the business. Frank died two years ago. He had moonshine money still hidden away until the time he died. Not having invested any of it except in the partnership, he didn't lose anything when the stock market tanked. His family lived well during the Depression. Al took over the Mattson farm. Deiter sold his interest back to the company and moved to California. I haven't heard from him in a while. I'm foreman of P.M. & N. Logging. Well, I was until I got drafted.

Once I lost my family deferment in 1942, I figured I may as well make the most of it and go to officer candidate school. The pay was higher. What I didn't know then, was that Kraut snipers try to pick off our officers first. If I had known that, I would have preferred to be Private First Class

Heinlein. Casualties among officers are higher than even the new replacements. Those poor bastards have no idea what they're doing when they get here. Damn, they can do the stupidest things to get themselves killed.

As far as Sarah and the boys know, I got some frostbite and have been on R&R since. Sort of forgot to tell them about the shrapnel in my side. They'd just worry for no reason. Hey, I've got Miss Schwartz looking after me.

When we win this thing I want to try to find my father's grave before I get shipped back. I don't know for sure, but I think he's buried around here somewhere. Maybe with some searching I'll be able to find it. If nothing else the Krauts keep good records.

Sure as hell hope I don't get planted over here myself. Buried in Germany near my father's grave, each of us killed in the same place while fighting different wars on different sides—wouldn't that be the cat's ass.

"Hello, Lieutenant."

"Hi, Doc. Hi, Miss Schwartz." I can't believe this guy is a doctor. He looks fifteen.

"Well Doc, how am I doing?"

"Let's take a look. Feet first. Miss Schwartz, your notes indicate evidence of improved circulation. Yes. Color is coming back nicely. Do you have much pain, Lieutenant?"

"Yeah. But it's mostly throbbing now."

"Good, good. Probably won't have to take those toes off after all."

"I'm glad to hear that!"

"We had to amputate toes or feet from about a dozen boys over the last couple of weeks." Who's he calling boys?

"At least they get to go home, Doc. How about me? I can't be much good to the army gimpy like this."

"The brass wants every able-bodied soldier ready for the push into Berlin. They don't want the Russians getting there first. Your circulation is improving. There is no reason you can't rejoin your unit."

"What about my side wound?"

"I cleaned that out the day you arrived. A small piece of shrapnel created an entry wound through muscle tissue in your side, nicked a rib, and came to rest in your liver. One piece. I got it all."

"What all did you do in there?"

"Nothing but extract the shrapnel. Some internal bleeding, but the liver heals itself. Not much for me to do but stitch you up. Our only concern now is infection. Roll over, let's take a look. Have you noticed any oozing, Miss Schwartz?"

"No Doctor, and no inflammation either."

"Well, it looks clean to me, too, Lieutenant. You're good to go. Miss Schwartz, prepare the medically 'fit for duty' paperwork for the Lieutenant and have him discharged back to his unit tomorrow. Good luck, Lieutenant."

"Thanks, Doc." He left. Miss Schwartz stayed.

"Miss Schwartz, is that guy a real doctor and not just some kid the army calls a doctor?"

"Oh, he's really a doctor. He graduated from Johns Hopkins and did his residency at Newark General. He's very smart and cute, too!"

"Why, Miss Schwartz, you're making me blush."

The next morning Miss Schwartz brought my uniform and personal belongings and placed them on the foot of my cot. She handed me a copy of the "fit for duty" form and said, "You're discharged, Lieutenant, and have orders to rejoin your men." After I dressed, she walked me to the hospital entrance and said, "You take care of yourself, Lieutenant."

"That's my plan. Thank you, Miss Schwartz. Can't say I enjoyed the stay, but I did enjoy your company. Maybe I will see you in Berlin."

She smiled, turned and went back in to attend to her remaining patients.

I gingerly stepped out the hospital door and onto the wooden pallet that served as an entry. I paused as my eyes adjusted to the light and looked out at the path of compacted snow. It led to the road in front of the hospital where a troop truck waited to take the healed-up GIs back to their units—and to snowdrift bivouacs, marching the rutted icy roads, and the perils of war. *Piece of cake for a Chickadee.*

Afterword

This, my first book, a historical fiction about an immigrant boy's experience working as a chickadee in a logging camp in 1921, began as a research project. The project launched when I read a reprint of a 1930s article from a western Wisconsin newspaper of a group of loggers who found a petrified body, presumably of a French explorer, inside a huge basswood tree they'd just cut down. I was intrigued by this story and began researching logging camp records, letters, memoirs, articles, and records at the University of Wisconsin where the body was purportedly sent. Who was this man in the tree? What events led him there? Who found him and when? All attempts at finding the answers to these questions met with dead ends. The research into early twentieth-century logging however, produced a wealth of colorful figures, stories, and events and later became the foundation for this book.

With the advent of the Internet, I was able to resume researching the story more thoroughly and expediently. I quickly found that the account was fabricated by an editor needing another two hundred words to fill a newspaper page. However, the time invested seeking evidence of the fictional man in the tree report proved fruitful nonetheless. The old newspaper articles, logging company records, loggers' memoirs, letters, and the transcripts of their interviews were rich in history, exploits, and colorful anecdotes. I found the information to be interesting and entertaining and thought others might as well. While this book is historical fiction, many of the character names and places within the story were taken directly from the historical documents, and the contemporary global/political events and timelines depicted in the book are historically accurate.

In one of the letters reviewed during the preliminary research, I encountered an anecdotal reference to a "chickadee" working in a logging camp, with a brief description of the job. The notion of a boy working in such a dangerous industry, living in primitive conditions, among a diverse array of men, in remote areas largely devoid of law and order, was intriguing.

I was unable to find credible first-hand descriptions or autobiographical accounts by former chickadees. This impaired writing a history and led to the transition of the work becoming a historical novel. The story takes place primarily in the north woods of Wisconsin during 1920 and 1921. The narrative entwines the fictional story of an eight-year-old boy within that period's rich historical context. The story meticulously incorporates the history of logging in Wisconsin, as well as the flu pandemic, Prohibition, World War I, and post-war American culture, specific to that time and place. The story adheres to the era's colorful language, rich history, characters, and Wild West atmosphere.

About the Author

Jim Bastian and his wife Carol were born, raised, met, and married in Wisconsin. Jim received a Bachelor's Degree from Michigan State University. Upon graduation, he taught high school history and psychology, but subsequently converted to capitalism, earned an MBA, and went on to have a thirty-year business career. Jim and Carol spend as much time at their vacation home in Forest County, Wisconsin, as they can.